Her heart just hit the spin cycle

Marlee folded her arms across her chest. "I don't want you to think you can buy your way into my good graces."

"You think I'm trying to seduce you with a washing machine and dryer? Believe me, I could do better than that." The heated way Troy's gaze caressed her confirmed he had it in his power to seduce her with more than gifts and gestures.

She remembered how close she had come to giving in to her desire for him the other night up on the bluff. She'd spent seven years trying to forget the way his touch, his kiss, the very brush of his skin against her own could make her feel, and within hours of their meeting again, it had all come rushing back.

Dear Reader,

I love stories about second chances—second chances at a job or with family, and especially second chances at love. I've made my share of mistakes and though none of them have had the severe consequences of the actions of Troy, the hero of this story, I like to think that sometimes we can make up for the past.

This story was also a chance to return to one of my favorite cities: Austin, Texas. It was fun to hang out for the duration of this story in this very special place. I hope you'll enjoy the visit also.

I always like to hear from readers. You can e-mail me at Cindi@CindiMyers.com or write to me in care of Harlequin Enterprises Ltd., 225 Duncan Mill Rd, Don Mills, Ontario, Canada, M3B 3K9. To find out more about me and upcoming books, visit my Web site at www.CindiMyers.com.

Best wishes,

Cindi Myers

The Father for Her Son
Cindi Myers

HARLEQUIN®

TORONTO • NEW YORK • LONDON
AMSTERDAM • PARIS • SYDNEY • HAMBURG
STOCKHOLM • ATHENS • TOKYO • MILAN • MADRID
PRAGUE • WARSAW • BUDAPEST • AUCKLAND

Recycling programs
for this product may
not exist in your area.

ISBN-13: 978-0-373-71612-8

THE FATHER FOR HER SON

www.eHarlequin.com

Printed in U.S.A.

ABOUT THE AUTHOR

Cindi Myers's mother always told her she was a late bloomer, which may account for her enduring belief that you're never too old to try something new and her faith in second chances. She lives in the mountains of Colorado with her husband, two spoiled dogs and a very large collection of books and yarn.

Books by Cindi Myers

HARLEQUIN SUPERROMANCE
1498—A SOLDIER COMES HOME
1530—A MAN TO RELY ON
1548—CHILD'S PLAY

HARLEQUIN AMERICAN ROMANCE
1182—MARRIAGE ON HER MIND
1199—THE RIGHT MR. WRONG
1259—THE MAN MOST LIKELY
1268—THE DADDY AUDITION

HARLEQUIN NEXT
MY BACKWARDS LIFE
THE BIRDMAN'S DAUGHTER

HARLEQUIN ANTHOLOGY
A WEDDING IN PARIS
  "Picture Perfect"

HARLEQUIN SIGNATURE SELECT
LEARNING CURVES
BOOTCAMP
  "Flirting With an Old Flame"

For Julie, Robyn, Emily and Cyndee—the Austin Gang

CHAPTER ONE

MARLEE BRITTON SCOWLED at her computer and debated giving the machine a hard smack on the side. But she knew from experience she'd only hurt her hand. The little hourglass on the screen would keep blinking at her, taunting her with the promise that things would eventually get moving again.

She massaged the bridge of her nose, fighting the first twinges of a headache, and glanced at the clock. Only eleven. There were hours left in the workday.

"Marlee, there's someone here to see you."

She looked up from a stack of employee time sheets, into her boss's worried face. The manager of the Crowne Towers Hotel in Austin, Texas, Simon Morgenroth was normally a cheerful man, but at the moment his expression was guarded—as though he was about to deliver bad news.

Marlee felt a quiver of uneasiness in the pit of her stomach. "Is something wrong?" She started to stand. "Who is it?" she asked. The tension around Mr. Morgenroth's mouth set off alarm bells in her head again. "Who's asking for me?" Marlee couldn't remember the last time she'd had a personal visitor at work—if she ever had.

An aura of fatherly concern clung to Mr. Morgenroth's portly, balding figure. His caring attitude elicited midnight confessions from hotel guests and grateful unburdening from his staff, though Marlee wasn't inclined to share details of her private life. "He wouldn't give me his name. He just insisted on talking to you." Mr. Morgenroth shook his head. "It's really none of my business, but he's a rough-looking fellow. If you want, I'll send him away."

"No, no. I'll take care of it." Marlee's apprehension increased. What rough-looking man would be asking for her? She gave Mr. Morgenroth what she hoped was a reassuring smile. "I'll talk to this man for a minute, and that'll be the end of it."

Her boss insisted on walking with her to the lobby. Seeing no way to deter him, she passed through the double doors leading from the office to the front desk, Mr. Morgenroth right behind her. But no one waited for her at the polished marble counter. "Perhaps he left," Mr. Morgenroth said.

The new day clerk, Trish, tucked a lock of her short red hair behind one ear and nodded toward the seating area at the far end of the lobby. "If you're looking for the hottie with the motorcycle helmet, he's over there," she said. She flashed a wide smile. "While you're at it, find out if there's any more like him at home."

Mr. Morgenroth frowned at Trish, and started to lead Marlee across the lobby, but his cell phone trilled. "Hang on while I take this call," he said.

"It's okay," Marlee reassured him. "I'm sure this won't take long." Whoever this guy was, she would just as soon deal with him alone.

She headed toward the set of plushly upholstered armchairs. All she could see as she approached was the back of a man's head, his thick dark hair curling up at the collar of his black leather jacket. She was almost beside her visitor before he turned to face her. "Hello, Marlee."

The low voice resonated deep inside her, as familiar as memory. She went absolutely still, her wildly pounding heart the only evidence she had not been turned to stone. It couldn't really be him… The man stood, dark eyes fixed on her—eyes she saw in her dreams sometimes. She swallowed hard, unable to tear her gaze away from him. The dreams were always happy; the panic that swept over her now only came afterward, when she was awake. "Troy!" she gasped.

He reached out as if to touch her and she instinctively jerked away. Anger flared in his eyes as he let his hand fall to his side. His gaze roamed up her conservative black skirt to her silk blouse. She could feel the heat of that gaze, warming every part of her.

"What are you doing here?" she asked. At one time, her whole world had revolved around Troy Denton. He was the first—and only—man she'd ever loved.

Then he'd left her in the worst possible way. A way he had to know she could never forgive.

His eyes remained locked to hers. "I came back for what's mine."

"No." Marlee took a step back. This was the last thing she needed. She had a good life now and she wouldn't let him disrupt it.

"I wrote you," he said. "Why didn't you answer my letters?"

What was the point in writing back to someone she never wanted to see again? "I threw them away," she said. All of them. Unopened. She'd believed a clean break was the only way to survive the pain, though a little piece of her had died every time a new envelope arrived.

Troy clenched his jaw. "You could have at least given me a chance to explain."

Why should I give you a chance? she wanted to ask. *You never gave* us *one.* But she was conscious of being in a public place, her coworkers looking on. "I don't have anything to say to you."

She turned away, afraid she might give in or let down her guard. She'd loved him so much—but no. That was a long time ago.

"How's Greg?"

Her breath rushed out of her. She swayed on her feet. "How do you know his name?"

She could see the hard lines around his eyes. He hadn't had those lines before. "My mom told me about him," he said.

She took another shaky step back, away from him. "I don't want to talk to you about Greg, or about anything else." Turning on her heel, she started across the lobby, but he caught her arm.

Her body leaned into his touch, even as her mind

told her to run. She felt the scrape of his callused hands on her sleeve, the warmth of his skin soaking into her through the silk.

"Don't go," he commanded, his voice a sensuous rumble, another weapon against her resolve. "We have to talk."

Emotion overwhelmed her, a great boiling rush of fury and longing and fear. "Nothing you can say or do will make up for what you did to me—what you did to me *and* Greg." She wrenched her arm loose. "We've gotten along just fine without you. We didn't need you then and we sure as hell don't need you now."

"Is this man bothering you, Marlee?"

She hadn't heard Mr. Morgenroth walk up behind her.

She shook her head, mortified. "No, I'm all right." She couldn't handle Mr. M. finding out about her former relationship with Troy.

"Marlee and I were having a private conversation." Troy glowered at Mr. Morgenroth.

Mr. Morgenroth turned to Marlee, a question in his eyes. She ignored it, pretending to study the pattern in the carpet. She hated having her troubles on display like this. She'd have given almost anything to be somewhere else.

"You can't come barging in here, interrupting Marlee at work," Mr. M. said. "No matter what she says, it's obvious you're upsetting her."

Troy looked at Marlee, as if he expected her to come to his defense. She averted her gaze and gave a small shake of her head. This wasn't the time or the place for this conversation. Talking wouldn't solve anything between them now.

The hotel security guard, Mike, approached. Trish or Mr. Morgenroth had probably summoned him when Troy had grabbed her arm. "We're going to have to ask you to leave," Mike said, putting his hand on Troy's shoulder.

Troy opened his mouth as if to speak, then shut it again. His gaze burned into Marlee and she shivered. She recognized the pain lurking behind his anger, and part of her wanted to go to him—to comfort him and to take comfort from him.

That the impulse was still there after so long disturbed her.

Troy shrugged off Mike's grip and started toward the door. "We'll talk later," he said over his shoulder, crossing the lobby in long strides.

Marlee fled to her office, where she collapsed in her chair. Why, after all these years, had Troy come back?

"Are you all right?" Mr. Morgenroth set a paper cup of water in front of her. Then he perched on the edge of the desk and stared down at her.

Her fingers trembled as she straightened the stack of time sheets in front of her. "Of course I'm fine." But her voice shook, betraying the lie.

"Who was that man?" her boss asked. "What did he do to upset you so much?"

The questions helped Marlee pull herself together, the familiar defense mechanisms falling into place. *Don't talk about yourself. Be vague and change the subject as quickly as possible.* "Oh—just an old friend. He was in town, thought he'd stop by and say hello." She tried to keep her tone light, but she could feel the tears clogging the back of her throat. *Why did you do it, Troy? Why did you mess things up between us when we were so good together?* And why had he come back now, just when she was building the life she'd always wanted for herself and her son?

"I'd better get back to work," she said, avoiding looking at her boss. "Nancy'll have my head if I'm late with the payroll figures."

Mr. Morgenroth stood and started to leave. She could feel him watching her from the door, but she forced herself to focus on the papers in front of her. She didn't want to invite more questions.

"Well, call me if you need anything," he said, and walked out of the office.

Marlee turned to her computer and tried to concentrate on entering the information from the time sheets. But memories of Troy Denton kept pushing their way into her thoughts, as insistent as the man himself.

She'd been the pushy one when they'd first met. Was there anything bolder than a seventeen-year-old girl who knew what she wanted? Her mother used to say Marlee was all hair and hormones. Back then, her brown hair had hung almost to her waist and her hormones had made all the decisions for her.

Common sense certainly had nothing to do with the way she acted around Troy back then. He had been older—twenty-two. The first time she'd laid eyes on him as she walked past the gas station where he worked, her stomach had done a funny flip-flop. His sleeves had been rolled up to reveal tanned, muscular arms, and his well-worn jeans had clung to slim hips. Troy Denton had been all man—not a boy like the guys at school.

She hadn't been looking for romance. She'd wanted to have a good time, and to assert her independence by dating a man her mother wouldn't approve of. Her father had been already out of her life by then, in prison where he belonged.

Marlee had started walking to the station every day after school. She'd told her mother she was going to buy a soda, but really she went to flirt with Troy. She could still remember the smells of grease and diesel that lingered around the mechanics' bays, and taste the fizzy orange soda from the machine by the garage door. She'd drink hers slowly, trying to catch Troy's eye as he worked.

At first, he'd hardly looked up from changing tires or cleaning batteries. But after a while he'd come out of the bay to talk to her. He'd seemed larger than life in her eyes—stronger, more handsome, more *masculine* than anyone she knew. She could have floated all day on one of his smiles.

Love had caught her by surprise, as had her mother's approval of Troy. "I'm glad you found a good man," her mother had said. "You won't make the same mistakes I did."

But time had proved them both wrong. Troy had been a huge mistake.

And now he was back. Marlee closed her eyes. So much about Troy was the same, from his coffee-brown eyes to his perfectly shaped body, muscular arms and slim hips.

So much about Troy was different, too. He seemed tougher, even menacing. Part of that may have been the black leather and the motorcycle helmet, but there was more than just that. The Troy she'd known before had been very relaxed and easy-going. The man she'd seen today had been deadly serious.

So why had he come back now? What did he want from her?

Greg? Her breath caught. Greg had no idea who his father was and Marlee meant to keep it that way. She'd even suffered the indignity of writing Unknown in the space for the father's name on his birth certificate—better that than admit in black and white that she'd once loved a man like Troy Denton.

What if Troy had come back to claim his son? What if he wanted to take Greg away from her? Marlee's first impulse was to run as fast and as far as she could. She'd take Greg and go somewhere Troy could never find them.

But her heartbeat gradually slowed and her senses cleared. Running away wouldn't solve anything. Especially when she didn't even know Troy's intentions. She forced herself to take a deep, steadying breath. She wasn't going to lose her son.

Troy said he'd come back for what was his. Was he talking about Greg? Her? If he contacted her again, as he'd said he would, she'd listen to his explanations. Words wouldn't change what he'd done, but the meeting would give her the opportunity to make clear that she wanted him out of her life, and out of her son's life.

MARLEE TRIED to focus on work, but shortly before three o'clock, she gave in to the headache that had been building all morning and asked if she could take off early. Mr. Morgenroth studied her a moment. "This doesn't have anything to do with that man who was here before, does it?" he asked.

"Of course not. I'm just a little tired." Which wasn't a complete lie. She'd already had a headache when Troy showed up, but he certainly hadn't helped.

Mr. M. shook his head. "I'm not sure I believe you, but by all means, go home and rest. Just remember—" he stopped her with a hand on her shoulder as she turned to leave "—if you need anything—if you're in some kind of trouble—you can always come to me."

Marlee nodded, then quickly left the office. She appreciated Mr. Morgenroth's concern, but there was nothing anyone could do. She'd have to handle this on her own—the same way she'd handled everything else for the past six years.

A few minutes later, she pulled into the parking lot of Waterloo Elementary School. She stood beside her car a moment and watched a group of children in the school's After-Care program scaling the ropeladdered sides of a fort on the playground. Greg had already reached the top platform. He leaned over the railing and shouted down to the children below. Marlee smiled and felt some of her gloom lift. How could she regret any of the choices she'd made when they'd brought her this child to love?

She'd certainly never intended to be a mother so young. She and Troy had tried to be careful, but just after her nineteenth birthday, she'd discovered she was pregnant.

When she'd finally worked up the courage to tell him that evening, he'd been as stunned as she was. "Wow. That's a surprise, isn't it?"

But before she could burst into tears, he'd put his arm around her. "We'll get married right away," he'd said. "It'll be great."

"Troy, what are we going to do for money?" she'd asked. Her job working the cash register at a little deli barely had covered her own bills, and Troy hadn't made much as a mechanic. "Babies are expensive."

"It'll work out," he'd said. "Something will turn up." That had always been Troy's philosophy in those days.

Marlee had believed in that philosophy, too, and she'd trusted Troy to look after her. She'd begun to let herself get excited, looked forward to being a mom and wife—Mrs. Troy Denton.

Then Troy had walked out the door and out of her life.

When she hadn't heard from him all the next day,

she'd gone to his house in the evening to talk to him. His mother had met her at the door. Sue Denton had never been very friendly to Marlee, so the scowl on her face hadn't been a surprise. But her words had been. "Troy ain't coming back," she'd said. "He made me promise not to tell you where to find him." Then she'd shut the door in Marlee's face.

Marlee clutched her stomach now, feeling the same wrenching sickness she'd felt that horrible day at Troy's mom's. It hadn't taken her long to discover what had happened to Troy. He had been arrested for taking part in a robbery in which a man had been shot.

Marlee's father had spent her whole life on the wrong side of the law. Frank Britton's wrongdoings had hurt Marlee and her mom more than she could begin to describe. To know Troy was following in her father's footsteps was the greatest betrayal she could imagine.

But maybe that hurt would prove valuable now that Troy was back in her life. It would remind her to be on her guard. She didn't want to risk losing Greg—or her own foolish heart—to him again.

Just then, Greg looked up and spotted her. He grinned and waved, then raced for the slide at the end of the platform. Marlee met him in the hall outside his classroom. "Hi, Mom!" he called, and threw his arms around her.

She returned the hug, then smoothed a lock of hair from his forehead. Greg had his father's hair, thick and black and unruly. He looked up at her with his father's eyes, the color of fudge and lively with intelligence. "How come you're here early?" he asked.

"Maybe I just wanted to see you." She slipped her arm around his shoulders and they walked into the room side by side. "I got off a little early," she said to Mrs. Ramirez, his teacher.

"No, she wanted to see me," Greg said. He raced for his locker.

"Don't forget your backpack," Marlee called.

"Here's some information about our open house next week." Mrs. Ramirez handed her a flyer. "We encourage all the parents to come. Grandparents, too."

Marlee nodded and stuffed the paper in her purse. She wouldn't bother explaining to Mrs. Ramirez that Greg's dad wouldn't be coming to the open house. His grandparents wouldn't, either. The teacher knew she was a single mom, but Marlee had deliberately kept other family details private, partly to avoid having Greg singled out as different. But it made her sad to think about their lack of family. And she didn't have time for sadness. "Come on, Greg, let's go."

On the drive home, Greg rattled on from the backseat about the fish in the aquarium at school and his friend Rachel's new front tooth and the story Mrs. Ramirez had read. Marlee listened with half an ear and thought about the father-daughter dance the Girl Scouts had given when she was in the fifth grade. She'd been the only girl in her class without a father, or at least a grandfather or uncle, to attend.

Plenty of mothers raise their children by themselves, she reminded herself. *Things are different now than they were when I was a kid.* She glanced in the rearview mirror and caught a glimpse of Greg, his face animated as he relived the exciting moment when Rachel had succeeded in wiggling free her loose tooth. Marlee tried to be a good mother, but was that enough? Did Greg need a dad also?

She hadn't dated since Troy left. At first she'd been too busy trying to put food on the table and diapers in the cupboard. Later, she'd been too afraid of making the same mistake again. She'd convinced herself she was better off on her own.

As she turned onto their street, Greg leaned forward in his seat. "Mom, who's that at our house?"

Marlee's mouth went dry as she took in the gleaming chrome-and-black motorcycle parked at the curb. A black helmet rested on the saddle seat. Something moved in the shadows on the front steps and a familiar figure in a black leather jacket stepped into the light.

CHAPTER TWO

"WHO IS THAT, MOM?" Greg asked again, now leaning as far forward as his seat belt would allow.

"A...a friend." Marlee tried to keep her voice from shaking. Troy looked so out of place in front of the house. It was *her* house—her private sanctuary she never shared with anyone but Greg.

Don't let him get to you, she told herself as she parked the car in the driveway. *Hear what he has to say and then he'll go. This will be over with soon enough.*

Troy waited on the steps for them to get out of the car. He stood with his feet apart, thumbs hooked in his front pockets, like a gunfighter waiting to face an adversary at high noon. The arrogance of his stance annoyed Marlee.

"Hello, Marlee. Hello, Greg." Troy's attention shifted to the boy. An expression of pure longing flashed across his face, quickly masked by a friendly, if cautious, smile.

Greg looked at him quizzically. "How did you know my name?"

Troy glanced at Marlee, a question in his eyes. She

frowned and shook her head. He turned back to the boy, his smile slightly strained now. "Your mom told me."

"What's your name?" Greg asked.

Troy crouched down until he was level with his son. "I'm Troy." He stuck out his hand. "Pleased to meet you."

Greg grinned and slid his small hand into Troy's work-roughened palm. Marlee fought a sudden tightness in her throat and had to look away. But the image lingered in her mind of the man and the boy, like two figures carved from the same block of stone.

"Is that your motorcycle?" Greg asked.

Troy nodded. "She's mine, all right."

"Would you take me for a ride?"

"Greg!" Marlee scolded, horrified at the thought of her little boy on a motorcycle, much less with Troy.

Troy chuckled and stood. "Not today. But maybe later I'll let you sit on it with me."

"Wow! That'd be great!"

"Greg, go inside and let me talk privately to Mr. Denton," Marlee said.

"Awwww, Mom!"

"You heard me, young man. You can watch TV in the den for a while."

Greg gave Troy a pleading look, as if some instinct told him another male would take his side. "Better mind your mom," Troy said.

Greg shrugged, and headed for the house. Marlee waited until he was inside before she turned to the man beside her. "Troy, please. Don't do this."

"I just want to talk, Marlee. To explain. Then if you still want me to leave, I will."

His words were humble, but his eyes held a challenge. *You're going to listen to me.*

Determined not to let him see how shaken she was, she started up the front steps, though she could still feel him watching her as she led the way into the house.

She walked straight to the kitchen, where she dumped her purse on the counter. "Would you like something to drink?" she asked, taking a pitcher of tea out of the fridge.

"Tea will be fine." He sat down at the table and looked around. The rental house was small and old—not her dream home. She was saving for a better place, but in the meantime, she'd done her best to make this one comfortable. She'd decorated the room in country blue and white, complete with ruffled curtains on the windows and a wallpaper border of ribbon-trimmed geese. Troy's masculinity was more overwhelming than ever in such surroundings.

She set a glass of tea in front of him, then took a seat across the table. "Say what you've got to say, then leave."

He stared at the tabletop, his hands spread out flat in front of him. She studied his long, square-tipped fingers—mechanic's fingers, crisscrossed with nicks and scars, strong enough to loosen stuck spark plugs or bend thick wire. But Marlee suddenly remembered how gentle those fingers could be, brushed across sensitive skin…

She blinked, a blush warming her cheeks at the unwanted memories. Raising her eyes, she met Troy's steady gaze. Her face grew hotter, and she feared he might read her thoughts.

But he betrayed no emotion beyond grim determination. "You didn't tell him, did you?"

Marlee glanced toward the kitchen door, but there was no sign of Greg. The television blared reassuringly from the living room. "I didn't think he needed to know."

"I'm sorry." His voice was low, the words strained. "I ran out on you when you needed me most." He curled his fingers into white-knuckled fists. "But you ran out on me, too. I think it's time we called it even and did what's best for Greg."

She flinched at the barely suppressed anger in his voice. Fine. He talked about doing what was best for Greg—why couldn't he understand that she'd done what she had to do to protect her son? "Why did you do it?" she asked. "Why—when you had so much to lose?"

"I did love you. I wanted a perfect life for us." He pushed his chair abruptly away from the table, rattling the glasses and making her jump. "Then I went and screwed it up."

"You made a choice. You chose to break the law— to go after easy money. And it cost you everything. It cost *us* everything." She remembered her anguish when she heard he'd been arrested. She'd thought he was a different kind of man. One she could trust. Learning the truth had broken her heart.

He lowered his gaze, refusing to look at her. "I did my time. I paid my debt and I won't do anything like that again."

He sounded sincere, but she'd heard that brand of sincerity before, from her own father, who broke every promise he made to go straight. "You say that now," she stated. "But why should I believe it?"

"Because whatever else I've done, I've never lied to you." His voice and his expression were hard. "I'm not a liar."

"I didn't think you were a thief, either."

Troy clenched his jaw, and his knuckles whitened as he gripped the glass. Marlee sucked in a breath, a cold sliver of fear piercing her anger. But as she watched, he took a deep breath, and his shoulders relaxed.

"I know I hurt you," he said. "But I'm back now. And I'm going to make it up to you. I've never stopped thinking about you these seven years—wondering how you were doing. Wondering what the baby was like."

"He's not a baby anymore." It was a cruel thing to say, deliberately reminding him of what he'd missed. But she wanted to hurt him, to make him pay for the way he'd hurt her.

"I'm going to take care of you now," he said. "I've got it all planned out."

The Troy she'd known before had never planned anything. He took each day as it came. At the time, his laid-back approach had delighted her. But this man wasn't laid-back in the least. He was all coiled tension. So certain and determined.

But she could be determined, too. "Greg and I don't need taking care of."

He opened his mouth to protest, then closed it again. He looked at her a long moment, as if searching for something in her expression. She wondered if she seemed different to him. She felt different—older, wiser, more self-sufficient and independent than she'd been years ago.

His already determined expression hardened even more. "A boy needs a father."

"Not one who's been in prison since before he was born!" Not a father like the one she'd grown up with.

"I didn't know my cousin was going to rob that liquor store," Troy said.

In those early days, Marlee had wanted to believe him. She'd somehow found the courage to go to the jail and visit him. She'd tried to stand by him despite her hurt and the fear that history was repeating itself. She'd worked so hard to make a life different from her mother's, yet here she was, pledging herself to a man who might end up like her father.

She'd remained strong until the end of the trial, when a jury found Troy guilty and sentenced him to prison. The evidence against him seemed so damning—how could he *not* have known what his cousin had planned? Troy admitted he'd approached his cousin about needing extra money for the baby—the fact that he'd broken the law for her somehow made the situation worse.

She'd walked out of the courtroom that day

intending to also walk away from the pain. She wouldn't be the jailhouse widow her mother had been, and she refused to make her baby a convict's child.

"You knew the kind of man your cousin was," she said now. "You made a choice. The wrong choice."

"I was stupid," Troy said. "And I'll never stop being sorry for what I put you through. Now that I'm out, I'm going to do right by you and Greg."

"My son isn't going to grow up with a criminal for a father," she insisted. "I want him to have a better life than I did." Her father had seldom been around when she'd needed him, but his reputation had hung over the family like a black cloud. Everyone in their neighborhood knew Frank Britton, and they didn't want their children playing with his.

Her son shouldn't have to deal with the stigma of a con—or even an ex-con—for a father.

Troy slid out of the chair and stood. "I can't change the past," he said. "We've got to think about the future now, and what's best for Greg."

Marlee stood, too, unwilling to give him the advantage of looming over her. "I won't let you hurt him," she said.

"He's my son. I have the right to see him."

Marlee froze at the words. "Is that a threat?" she asked.

"I'll do what I have to do," he said. "I'll take you to court if I need to."

The prospect of that kind of expense and the shame of having their history out in the open made her feel faint. "He doesn't know anything about you," she said. "What's he going to think if you just drop into his life now after being gone so many years? How are you going to explain where you've been?"

"We won't tell him the whole story right away. It doesn't matter where I've been, anyway. What matters is that I'm here now."

"No. You'll confuse him."

"I'm his father!" His voice rose, sharp with anger. "How could you keep that from him?"

She had no argument to combat that truth. No words that would make this situation—and Troy—go away.

"You should get to know him first," she said. "Then, when he's more used to you, we can tell him." Maybe.

"I don't like lying to him."

"And I won't have him hurt by the truth."

He stood in front of her, towering over her. He was huge. The shoulders she'd so often rested her head on in the past now seemed more powerful, almost menacing. She missed the comfort she used to find in sharing her burdens with him. But she wasn't that weak anymore. She didn't need him.

He put his hand on her shoulder. His grasp was heavy and warm; the heat seemed to travel down her arm to the rest of her body. "Do it for Greg," he said.

"I *am* thinking of Greg. He and I have a good life together. He's happy. You'll only upset him."

"A boy needs a father," Troy insisted. "What are you going to do when he's a teenager, asking about his father, and you have to tell him you sent me away? What will that do to him?"

Marlee flinched. Was he right? Boys were different from girls, and already she worried Greg needed a male influence. One day, probably sooner rather than later, Greg would want to know about his father, the real story, not the reassurances that he didn't have a father. He was still young enough to believe it, but as soon as he figured out biology, he'd realize a man had to have been involved.

And here was Troy—refusing to give up or go away. He hadn't said he'd make trouble if she didn't let him see Greg, but the unspoken threat was there. She took a deep breath. "All right. But we'll go slow. You can visit, but only if I'm here with you." She looked him in the eye. "And you can't tell him you're his father. Not until I decide the time is right."

"I told you before—I'm not a liar. I won't lie to my son."

"I'm not asking you to lie, just not tell the whole truth. Not until I'm sure he's ready."

Anger flared in his eyes, but he quickly masked it. "If that's the only way…"

"It is."

He took a step back. "Mind if I show him my motorcycle?"

Greg came tearing out of the den the minute Troy called his name. Marlee stayed on the front steps as Troy straddled the bike and helped Greg climb in front of him. Greg was all little-boy innocence, beaming with delight as he fiddled with controls and thumped his heels against the bike's gas tank.

An air of danger clung to Troy like the leather jacket that hugged his muscular back and shoulders. He stroked the gleaming machine the way a man might caress a beautiful woman—equal parts love, pride and possession. Marlee remembered again how his hands had stroked her with that same mastery.

Greg said something that made Troy laugh, lighting his face with mirth. She gasped slightly and pressed one hand to her chest, as if to calm her rapid heartbeat. This was the Troy she'd missed, the laughing, handsome man she'd loved. It unnerved her to think he was still there inside this other man, the solemn fugitive who had betrayed her. It would be too easy to fall in love with this hidden Troy all over again.

That love doesn't exist anymore, she reminded herself. And she wasn't about to rekindle it. She was strong enough now to resist that temptation. She wouldn't allow him to break her heart twice.

TROY OPENED the throttle wide and raced the motorcycle down the straightaway toward Lake Austin. The wind buffeted his helmet, almost drowning out the whine of the bike. If only he could drown out the voice in his head, the one that shouted he was a fool for coming back.

He flipped on his blinker and turned onto Mount Bonnell Road, leaning the bike into the curve until he was in danger of laying it down. But the rush he craved, that dizzying feeling of pumping adrenaline, eluded him today. Risking his life seemed tame compared to the risks he'd already taken with his heart.

Downshifting, he cut the engine and coasted into Mayfield Park. He parked the bike, then pulled off the helmet and walked to a picnic table. He thought about sitting down, but continued to the edge of the water instead.

He hadn't slept for two nights, working up the courage to talk to Marlee. Then when he saw her in the lobby of that fancy hotel, he'd almost lost his nerve. She was so beautiful—more beautiful than he remembered.

He'd spent seven years torn between memories of how much he'd loved her and anger that drove him to hate her. When she'd walked away after his trial, she'd taken so much from him—hope and dignity. She'd also taken his son.

His only goal when he'd been released had been to reclaim his boy. He told himself that Marlee's feelings for or against him no longer mattered. He didn't blame her for hating him. He'd expected she would.

But he hadn't anticipated how much it would hurt to see disdain in eyes that had once looked at him with love.

It didn't help that his body refused to acknowledge any bad blood between them. Alone with her in her kitchen, he'd had to fight himself to keep from pulling her into his arms. For a moment he'd even imagined she felt the same powerful attraction.

Of course she wasn't the same. He wasn't the same. He'd been a fool to think she'd wait for him, especially when he'd given her no reason to do so.

His eyes felt gritty. He rubbed a hand over his face and noticed he needed a shave. *Great. I probably look like some derelict. That probably didn't help convince Marlee to let me see Greg.*

"Greg. My son." He said the words out loud. He could still feel the boy's weight in his arms as he'd helped him on and off the bike. Troy closed his eyes and inhaled deeply. Underneath the mud and fish odors of the lake he imagined he could still smell the little-boy scents of soap and peanut butter.

The sun sat on top of the water like an orange balanced on a silver platter. Troy took another deep breath and studied the colors painting the clouds. He'd missed this. Seven years was an eternity to be away.

He'd been out of prison a month now—long enough to find a job and a place to live. He'd wanted at least the trappings of a normal life in place before he approached Marlee. It had taken him only a week to find her; she lived just a few blocks from the house she'd grown up in. He'd told himself it was a good sign that she wasn't making any effort to hide.

When she hadn't answered any of his letters, he'd been hurt, then angry. She'd been carrying his child. Hadn't that meant anything?

Over time, his anger had cooled. He knew how Marlee felt about her father. No matter how much he protested he wasn't like Frank Britton, why should she believe him?

He'd kept writing to her, just in case she was reading the letters, and he'd vowed when he got out he'd come back and prove to her he would be the man she needed. He would be a father to their son.

"IS TROY GOING to come back to see us soon, Mom?"

Marlee glanced in the rearview mirror as she drove home from the school the next afternoon. Greg grinned back at her in the reflection. "I…I don't know," she said. The same question or variations of it had rattled around in her head for the past twenty-four hours. Troy had seemed very determined to be a part of his son's life yesterday, but how could she be sure? Troy was virtually a stranger to her now.

"I really like him. That was a cool motorcycle he had. *Vrrroom. Vrrroom.*" Greg pantomimed revving a motorcycle's engine. "I'm going to have one just like it one day."

"Oh, you are, are you?" She shuddered at the thought of Greg racing around town on a motorcycle. "Well, it'll be a long time before you're old enough for that."

"Maybe Troy will take me riding." She heard more engine noises from the backseat.

Greg hadn't stopped talking about Troy since meeting him yesterday afternoon. Marlee tried to reassure herself that maybe it was the motorcycle, not the man, that had made such an impression. He wouldn't be too hurt, then, if Troy never came back.

What about her? How would she feel if she never saw Troy again? Relieved, she decided. She could get back to the routine of her life without him. His coming here had forced her to unearth a lot of old feelings that were best kept buried.

She had made a good life for herself and Greg without Troy's help, a life she could be proud of, with a good job and savings and a comfortable home. She wasn't where she wanted to be yet, but she was getting there, and she didn't want Troy pulling her back into a world she'd fought so hard to escape—a world of uncertainty and risk and loss of respectability.

She stopped at a traffic light and reached up to rub the back of her neck. She hadn't slept well. Questions kept tumbling in her brain like sneakers in a dryer. What did Troy want from them?

"Hey, Mom!"

Marlee jerked out of her daze at Greg's summons. She looked up and noticed the light was green. "What is it, Greg?" she asked as she got the car moving again.

"Maybe we could invite Troy for dinner. I bet he'd like that."

"Oh, Greg, I don't know…"

"You could call him when we get home." Greg sounded pleased with himself.

"I don't know his phone number." In fact, she knew no more about Troy than she had before yesterday afternoon, except that he was out of jail. If he cared that much about them, why didn't he at least leave his number, or an address?

"Well, you'd better ask him when he comes to see us again."

Greg was so sure Troy would be back, but she didn't have that childlike faith. She felt old and jaded.

Her stomach tensed as their house came into view and she saw the motorcycle once more parked at the curb. A second later, Greg shouted from the backseat. "Mom, he's here! Troy's here!"

"I can see that," she said. She doubted her words even registered with the boy. He was bouncing up and down in his booster seat, the seat belt straining to contain him. As soon as the car had come to a complete stop in the driveway, Greg was out of his seat and hurtling toward the man waiting on the porch. "You're back!"

Troy's grin was as wide as Greg's. He swept the boy into his arms and hugged him close. Marlee glimpsed some kind of uniform shirt under his leather jacket, as if he'd just come from work. But he'd obviously taken the time to shave; his jaw was smooth, without a hint of five-o'clock shadow. "I thought you and your mom might like to go out for pizza," he said to Greg.

Marlee shook her head. "I don't know—"

"Yeah! Pizza!" Greg's cries of glee quickly drowned out her objections.

Troy smiled at her over Greg's head. "Come on, Marlee. A little pizza won't hurt."

There'd been a time when a smile like that would have made her weak in the knees and light-headed with happiness. The fact that it could still make her a little wobbly and uncertain only angered her now. She fished her keys from her purse and slipped past

Troy to unlock the door. "Greg, put your backpack away," she ordered.

For once the boy didn't argue, though his slumped shoulders and shuffling walk let her know what he thought of her interrupting his happy reunion with Troy.

She heard Troy behind her as she entered the kitchen, his boot heels striking hard on the vinyl flooring. The sound annoyed her. She hadn't invited him in, had she? He had no right to be here.

She turned to tell him so, and discovered she was trapped. Troy stood in the narrow doorway, his body an imposing barrier to any escape. Arms outstretched, he gripped the counter on either side of the entrance and leaned toward her. "What is it?" he demanded. "What's wrong?"

She pulled a glass from the cabinet, then busied herself filling it from the tap. "Don't think I don't know what you're doing."

"What do you mean? I asked you and Greg out for pizza." Marlee could hear the barely contained frustration in his voice.

She set the glass down hard on the counter and faced him once more. "You knew I couldn't say no without upsetting Greg. You're already taking advantage of him."

He let out a deep breath and raked a hand through his hair. "Taking advantage of him? I asked you out for *pizza!* I just thought it would be good to do something together and I figured, well, we all have to eat."

"You thought it would be good, did you? What about what *I* think?" She refused to allow him to waltz in here after seven years and turn her life upside down. "Did you even consider I might have other plans for the evening? That Greg might have homework or chores? That we have a routine you're disrupting?"

"It's one night," he argued. "One dinner. I just want to spend time with my son."

He wouldn't beg, but there was no disguising the longing in his voice. And the determination. If she was to stay in control of this new relationship between them, she had to take charge now. "We're going to have to set some rules," she said.

Troy narrowed his eyes. "Whose rules?"

"Mine. First of all, if you want to see us, you call. Don't just show up on my doorstep. I don't like surprises."

He raised one eyebrow. "You used to. Like surprises, that is." His voice was low and teasing.

Marlee tried to ignore the tremor that burned through her. "That was a long time ago," she said. "I've changed."

He kept his expression neutral, giving nothing away. "Go on."

She glanced at the phone on the wall behind him. "Call me at work so you won't upset Greg."

"*I'm* not the one upsetting Greg now," he grumbled under his breath.

She ignored him, and continued. "Second, you will see Greg no more than twice a week, and only one school night. He gets too excited when you're around."

He took a step toward her, shrinking the gap between them. She backed up against a spice rack mounted on the wall.

"What about you, Marlee?" he asked. "Do you get too excited when I'm around? Is that the real reason you don't want to see me more often?"

"Of...of course not!" But the shakiness in her voice betrayed how much he *did* upset her. She swallowed hard, refusing to meet his eyes, afraid she might lose herself in them. "We aren't talking about you and me," she said, trying again.

"We aren't?" He moved another step closer to her. Only a few inches separated them. She felt the edges of the spice tins dig into her back as she pressed her body more firmly against the rack.

She took a deep breath, drawing in the erotic fragrances of male musk mingled with cinnamon. "Th-this isn't about us," she stammered. "This is about Greg."

"Greg *is* about us. He's *our* son. Nothing that's happened can change that." He stared at her, challenging her to deny the truth. "You've stated your rules, now it's my turn. Rule number one—you let me get to know Greg in my own way. I understand you want to chaperone, but don't tell me what to do around him. Number two—we need to try to be friends for his sake. You may hate me, but I'd rather he didn't know that."

"I don't hate you."

"You don't?" Troy shook his head. "You sure have an odd way of showing it." He reached out, as if to touch her cheek, and she flinched. "What are you afraid of?"

"I'm not afraid," she said, still not looking at him.

One finger brushed her cheek, sending prickles of sensation through her. "You're as jumpy as a cat," he said. "Are you scared of me—or of yourself?"

He brought his other hand up, as if to cradle her face. She cried out and darted through the gap between his side and the counter. "We'd better go," she said. Then louder: "Greg, what's taking you so long? Why aren't you changed yet?"

Greg appeared in the doorway, his jeans unzipped, clutching an Austin Ice Bats jersey to his naked belly. "I was looking for my shirt," he said. Greg had been devoted to the beleaguered minor league hockey team ever since a group of players had visited his school.

Marlee frowned at the wrinkled garment in his hand. A streak of dirt showed on the sleeve. "Where did you get that?"

He ducked his head. "The clothes hamper."

"You need to find a clean one."

"But I want *this* one. It's my favorite."

"It's also dirty." Marlee plucked the offending shirt from his hand. "You'll have to wait until Saturday to wear it again."

Greg scowled. "I hate going to the Laundromat on Saturdays," he said.

"I'm not exactly crazy about it myself," she said.

"But we have to have clean clothes. Now get another shirt and we'll go eat pizza."

The prospect of pizza seemed to cheer the boy. He raced back toward his room. Marlee turned to find Troy studying them. "Don't you have a washer and dryer here?" he asked.

"We've got the hookups, but not the machines." She folded the shirt and laid it on the counter. "There are other things that are more important for us to have right now." She was saving her money for a down payment on a nicer house in a better neighborhood. Everything else could wait.

He looked around the kitchen, as if seeing it for the first time. Marlee tried to picture what he saw: the broken hinge on one cabinet, the cracked windowpane over the sink, the watermark on the ceiling. Did he also see the ruffled curtains she'd made to hide the cracked pane, the cheery wallpaper and the silk flowers on the table? Did he recognize how hard she was trying to make a home? "Greg and I don't need fancy things," she said defensively. "We've got each other—that's what counts."

His eyes met hers and the anger in them chilled her. "Right," he said, and stalked past her. She heard his footsteps echo down the hall, then the door slammed behind him, hard enough to rattle the pictures on the wall.

Marlee sagged against the counter, worn-out from the emotion Troy had wrung from her. Obviously, he was angry that she wouldn't let him rush head-long into a no-holds-barred relationship with his son. But

she had to protect Greg, no matter what Troy
thought. The old Troy—the man she'd loved—had
never had this dark, bitter side to him. She needed to
remind herself of that next time she found herself
wishing they could re-create the past.

CHAPTER THREE

TROY WAS WAITING when Marlee and Greg emerged from the house. He lounged against her car, long legs stretched out in front of him, arms folded across his chest. In spite of her resolve not to, Marlee couldn't help but compare him with the young man she'd first seen at the service station near her house.

If anything, he was more handsome now. Maturity had filled out his wiry body and added solid muscle. His hair was shorter than he'd worn it then, the shorter cut accenting the hard line of his jaw. The curls on top were still untamed, falling boyishly over his forehead. But the dark eyes no longer held the innocence of youth. Instead, they were the eyes of a troubled man.

"I'll drive," he said, and scooped the keys from her hand.

Marlee started to protest, then thought better of arguing in front of Greg. "All right," she said, and opened the passenger door.

She was quiet on the drive to the pizza place, letting Greg and Troy do the talking. It was strange being next to Troy in the car. For one thing, she felt as if she was sitting too far over. Back when she and Troy had dated, they'd always sat close to each other. Sometimes he'd rest one hand on her knee, a protective, possessive gesture.

She took a deep breath, trying to steady herself, but all she could smell was Troy's leather-and-oil scent. The masculine odor evoked memories of the nights they'd spent together.

She crossed her arms in front of her, trying to squeeze out the shiver of remembered arousal. If she'd been dating regularly, would Troy's presence have raised such conflicting feelings within her?

They chose a booth at the restaurant. Greg insisted on sitting beside Troy. They'd just taken off their jackets and settled in when a waitress brought the menus over. "Welcome to the Pizza Pirate," she said, flashing a hundred-watt smile. "My name's Wendy and I'll be your server. Just let me know if you need anything."

Wendy was maybe all of sixteen, as pretty and vivacious as Marlee had been at that age. Marlee felt ancient in comparison. Did Troy notice how much she'd changed?

They ordered their drinks and Greg put in his vote for a large pizza with everything. "Sounds good to me," Troy said, returning his menu to Wendy.

"Fine with me." Marlee passed over her menu and the waitress swished away.

"Do you think she's cute?" Greg asked.

Marlee stared at her son. He was too young to be noticing girls, wasn't he? She glanced at Troy, who looked as if he was trying not to laugh. "Well, now,

I'd say so," he said. "Not as cute as some, but cuter than others." He winked at Marlee.

She felt herself blushing and was grateful when Troy turned his attention back to the boy. "What did you think?" he asked.

Greg drew himself up straight, his expression serious as he considered the question. "She was okay," he said after a moment. "But I like brown hair better."

"Well, what do you know," Troy said. "So do I."

Marlee put one hand to her brunette strands, then jerked it away when she noticed Troy watching her.

"Can I have some quarters for the video games?" Greg asked.

"How about if I play with you?" Troy said.

"Yeah. That'd be cool."

The waitress brought the tray of drinks and Marlee sipped her Diet Coke, wishing she'd ordered something stronger to steady her nerves. She couldn't believe she was letting Troy affect her like this.

I just have to figure out the proper way to act toward him, she told herself. Though she still didn't like it, she'd had no choice but to allow Troy to see Greg. For her son's sake, she couldn't stay angry with his father. But she couldn't pretend she'd forgiven him, either. She had to find some compromise, a friendly distance that acknowledged their connection through Greg, nothing more.

TROY LEANED against the video-game console and watched Greg annihilate the Gorgon Forces of Evil.

But his attention was repeatedly drawn to the woman across the room. Marlee sat with her back rigid, head high. She used her pride like a shield, keeping him at a distance. She had every right to be proud. She'd had to raise their son alone, and she'd done a great job, as far as he could tell. It couldn't have been easy—the shabby house told him a lot about the sacrifices she made.

He couldn't change what he'd done. He couldn't take away the pain of the past seven years for either of them. But he could make amends now. He'd give Marlee the things she'd denied herself and prove to her she didn't need to do everything on her own anymore. He would be there for her, and this time he wouldn't leave.

He looked down at his hands, at the grease tattooed into every line and crevice of his mechanic's fingers. No amount of scrubbing could get them completely clean. It wasn't only his body that was stained—he felt soiled inside by all the things he'd experienced in the past seven years. He'd seen men killed in prison fights and others who'd killed them-selves rather than live behind bars. He'd been stripped and searched and counted and reduced to a number instead of a human being. Only thoughts of Marlee and their son had kept him sane. They'd given him a purpose and a goal.

He glanced at Greg, so absorbed in the video game. Troy had already proved himself no match for the boy when it came to defeating animated foes. "I'll be at the table with your mother," he said.

Greg nodded, his eyes fixed on the screen, both hands working the joystick.

Troy slid into the booth next to Marlee. "Greg's a great kid," he said. "You've done a terrific job."

The compliment apparently caught her off guard. Her expression softened. "Thanks. He *is* a great kid."

"What did you tell him about me? I mean, about his father?"

She stared down at the red-and-white plastic tablecloth. "I told him his father left before he was born. We don't talk about you much."

He wanted to remind her that he hadn't left willingly, that it had all been a terrible mistake. But he knew from her earlier accusations that she didn't agree. In her view, he'd chosen to break the law and leave them—the same choice her own father had made too many times.

Knowing she lumped him into the same category as a career felon like Frank Britton angered and frustrated him. Words wouldn't be enough to convince her. He'd have to prove himself to her, maybe over and over again, but he'd do it. He'd learned a lot about patience in prison.

"Where are you working now?"

He welcomed the change of subject, and the chance to have a real conversation with her—maybe one that didn't end in an argument. "Wiley's." He tapped at the patch on the pocket of his shirt. "It's a custom-motorcycle shop."

"Have you been there long?"

He knew what she really wanted to know—had

he been back in town long? Had he been out of prison long? "No. About three weeks before I came to see you." It had taken him only a week to find the job, thanks to a referral from his parole officer.

Marlee stirred the ice in her glass with her straw.

"What about you?" he asked. "How long have you worked at the Crowne Towers?"

"Six years. I started there a few months after Greg was born. I worked at night and Greg stayed with my mom."

"What do you do there?"

"I'm an administrative assistant." She'd started at the front desk—the job Trish held now—and worked her way up.

"How is your mom?" He remembered Leigh Britton as a small, brown-haired woman who'd gone out of her way to avoid attracting attention to herself. She'd hidden from public censure and her husband's notoriety, even as she refused to turn her back on Frank, as Marlee had done.

When Troy had been arrested, he hadn't called Marlee. He knew how she felt about her father and about jails. He'd hoped to make bail and avoid having her see him behind bars. But the D.A. had other ideas. When Marlee had finally come to him, Troy had been elated; when she'd walked away that last time, he'd been crushed. Now he wondered if she'd only been trying to avoid her mother's sad fate, tied to a man who spent so much of his life locked away.

"She died two years ago. Cancer."

He winced. "Marlee, I'm sorry." One more thing he hadn't been around to help her through.

"Thanks. I...I still miss her." She glanced at him. "What about your mom?"

"She's got a job out at the mall. Works in the food court. She and I don't talk much these days." Rather, he didn't talk much to his mother. She still had plenty to say to him, most of it critical, of him and of Marlee. She blamed Marlee for everything that had gone wrong in his life. The way she saw it, if he hadn't gotten involved with Marlee, he wouldn't have approached Raymond and wouldn't have ended up in jail.

"She wasn't very nice to me, after...after you left."

He nodded, and took a long drink of his iced tea. His stomach churned when he thought of how cruel his mother might have been to Marlee. "What about your dad?" he asked. "What's he up to these days?"

She stiffened and set her mouth in a hard line. "How should I know?"

"Things haven't changed, then?"

She rubbed her thumb along the rim of her glass. "Why should they?"

"Do you know where he is now?"

She shrugged. "No, and I don't care."

"He might be out of prison. Maybe he's reformed."

"I'm not holding my breath."

"People can change."

She glared at him. "Why are you taking his side? You know how much he hurt me."

He could feel her pain washing over him in waves. He'd hoped by now those old wounds would have healed. He chose his words carefully. "Still…he's your father. The only family you have—"

"I have Greg. I don't need anyone else."

She didn't say *I don't need you,* but he was sure she thought it.

The pizza arrived, Greg trailing after the waitress like a hound tracking a rabbit. The boy saved him and Marlee from any further serious conversation. They confined themselves to a debate over pepperoni versus Canadian bacon and whether *Shrek* was a better movie than *Wall-E*.

"What do you think, Troy?" Greg asked.

Troy shifted in his seat. "Well, to be honest, I wouldn't know. I haven't seen either one of those movies."

"You're kidding! Why not?"

"Too busy, I guess." He glanced at Marlee, then quickly away, unnerved by how intensely she was studying him. "Now, baseball—there's a subject I'm an expert on."

They launched into a discussion of teams and players. Troy discovered he was enjoying himself. Greg was a bright kid, fun to be with. He'd accepted Troy's friendship so readily—if only Marlee could do the same.

It was fully dark by the time they left the restaurant, and Greg's head was already beginning to nod. Troy switched on the radio and the strains of soft rock filled the car. He recognized a song that had been popular when he and Marlee were dating. Maybe that was the key to reaching her—he would remind her of happier times.

He turned the car onto the road that ran by the lake.

Marlee jerked her head around. "Where are you going?"

"It's such a beautiful night. I thought we could take a drive."

He felt her watching him, but she remained silent. After a moment, she sank back against the seat, arms folded across her chest. Troy heard a child's soft snores behind him.

He drove onto a bluff high above the lake. The park there had been a popular make-out place years ago. Marlee must have recognized it, too. She sat up straight, but again, said nothing.

He parked at the scenic overlook. Switching off the engine, he stared out at a scene that had scarcely changed in seven years. A single security light cast a soft pink glow over the lot, which was empty except for their car. He rolled down the window and inhaled the loamy scent of lake water. "I think Greg's asleep," he said softly.

"It's past his bedtime."

Troy didn't miss the note of censure in Marlee's voice, but he refused to be drawn out of his mellow mood. He opened the car door. "Come sit with me a minute. We'll hear him if he wakes up."

"We should go home," she said, but followed him outside anyway.

He stepped up on the bumper and sat on the hood, then offered her his hand. She hesitated only a moment before taking it. "Do you remember when we used to come here?" he asked when she sat beside him, close, but not touching him.

She stared silently out at the dark water below.

Troy leaned back on his elbows and gazed up at the stars. "I remember this place," he said. Once they had made love here, entwined in the backseat of his car, too eager for each other to wait for a more private location. He turned to her. Her head was bent, and she kept her hands at her sides. "Tell me what you're thinking," he said.

She met his eyes, confusion apparent on her face. "I don't know you anymore, Troy. I'm not sure I want to."

"I'm not so different." He slid closer to her.

"But you are." She wet her lips. The sensuous gesture made his heart pound. "You're…more serious than you were before."

"I'm older, Marlee. We both are. We aren't ignorant kids." He rubbed his hand up and down her sleeve.

She leaned toward him, lips slightly parted in silent invitation. For seven years, he'd dreamed about her kisses—

"You're right, we're not kids." She pulled away and slid off the hood. "We have responsibilities. And mine is to get Greg home and to bed at a decent hour." She walked around to the passenger door without looking at him. "We'd better go now."

He stared after her, his body still craving her kiss while his mind tried to register her rejection. Biting back a sharp retort, he slid to the ground and got in the driver's seat. Without another word, he started the car and backed out of the overlook. So much for nostalgia. Things would never be the same between him and Marlee again. He might as well quit thinking they ever could be.

CHAPTER FOUR

ALL THROUGH BREAKFAST the next morning, Greg talked about Troy. "He loves pepperoni pizza, just like I do"…"Troy said I could probably beat him at video games—isn't that funny?"…"Troy said he'd watch *Wall-E* with me sometime, since it's my favorite movie."

Marlee wanted to cover her ears to keep from hearing Troy's name over and over. Greg's fascination reminded her of how close she'd come last night to falling under Troy's spell. At the park after dinner, sitting beside him in the darkness, memories of how he'd once made her feel had flooded her. Though she knew getting involved with him again would be a very bad idea, her body had other ideas. Every time he touched her, heat coursed through her, and when he leaned toward her, she longed for his kisses.

"I can't believe Troy hasn't seen *Shrek*," Greg said as he chased down the last frosted Oaty-oh in his bowl. "I've never met anyone who hasn't seen *Shrek*."

Greg's comment reminded Marlee of the reason Troy hadn't seen the popular movie—the reason she needed to guard against allowing physical desire to overwhelm common sense. "There's a lot of things we don't know about Troy," she said. "You need to be careful."

A sharp *V* formed between Greg's eyes—the same *V* Troy had when he was concentrating hard. "What do you mean, be careful?"

"You remember what I've always told you about not getting in cars with strangers or accepting presents from them."

"But Troy's not a stranger!" Greg's voice rose in indignation. "He's my friend." He carried his empty cereal bowl to the sink, then gave his mother a look of disdain that she'd never seen before. She wanted to hold him, to remind him how much she loved him and that they didn't need anyone else.

Instead, she let him leave the room, and fought down a wave of anger and, yes, jealousy. She and Greg had always been so close, a family of two. Troy had no right to take that away from her.

By the time they went out to the car Marlee had begun blaming herself for Greg's fascination with Troy. She'd kept Greg too sheltered, too much in her company, when he clearly needed some male attention. Greg wouldn't be so fascinated with Troy if he weren't the first man who'd spent any time with him.

"There's a program called Big Brothers," she said as she drove toward Greg's school. "It matches boys like you with a man who'll take you to the movies or play ball and do guy stuff. What do you think? Would you like to sign up for that?"

"I could play ball and do guy stuff with Troy."

"Troy might be too busy," she said.

"Let's ask him."

"But the man from this program would be specially matched to you—to be your big brother."

"I want to ask Troy first."

She ground her teeth together in frustration. Apparently no unknown "big brother" could compete with the man who'd come roaring into their lives on a motorcycle.

BY THE TIME Marlee arrived at work, she was determined not to think about Troy for the rest of the day. That resolution was dashed when she entered the break room and found Trish waiting for her.

The newest staff member at the hotel, Trish was only a couple of years younger than Marlee. She had a friendly, outgoing personality that was perfect for dealing with the public and was a marked contrast to the dour young man who'd held the desk clerk position previously. Though the two women were still getting to know each other, they were on their way to being friends—or as friendly as Marlee's carefully cultivated reserve would allow.

"See any more of Mr. Dark and Dangerous?" the clerk asked.

"Mister who?" Marlee moved past the younger woman to the coffeepot.

"That good-looking guy with the motorcycle who came by here the other day," Trish said. "I thought maybe the two of you were dating."

"Why would you think that?" Marlee asked. "The only time you saw him, we were arguing."

Trish shrugged. "I figured, you know, lovers' quarrel. There was just something about the way you two looked at each other."

"Well, you were wrong."

She wasn't sure how to explain her relationship with Troy. She couldn't call him just a friend, but they definitely weren't dating.

"Too bad. I could really go for a guy like that." Trish sat at the small table by the refrigerator and stirred sugar into her cup.

Trish could go for any guy. She was an admitted flirt. Marlee took the chair across from her. "His name's Troy. Mr. Morgenroth thought he looked rough."

"I like a guy who's a little rough around the edges."

"Why is that?" Marlee asked.

"Well…" Trish tapped the plastic stir stick against the side of her cup. "It's sexy. And I guess a guy like that—who hasn't lived an easy life—seems like the kind of man you could depend on to protect you if things got really rough."

"I don't need a man to protect me," Marlee countered.

"Maybe not. But it's nice to think he *would,* isn't it? It doesn't make us weak to want that, does it?"

"I don't know. Maybe it does."

"That's because you're a single mom," Trish said. "You can't afford to ever let your guard down. Me— sometimes I want to be taken care of." She laughed.

"Too bad I haven't found a guy who'll pamper me in the style I deserve."

"Better to work hard so you can pamper yourself," Marlee said.

"Yeah. I guess that way at least you know you'll get what you want." A blast of tinny hip-hop music jolted Trish upright. "Sorry. Got to take this call," she said, and slipped her phone out of her pocket.

Marlee returned to the open office space she shared with Mr. Morgenroth, her mind racing. She wondered what kind of life Trish had lived, that she was concerned about protection.

Would it surprise her to know how familiar Marlee was with violence and trouble?

Mr. M. thought Troy looked rough, but he had nothing on Marlee's father. When she was six years old, she'd been awakened in the middle of the night by shouts from the living room. She'd crept down the hall and watched as her father fought another man, pounding him with punch after punch until the other guy crumpled at his feet. Her father, one eye already swollen shut, blood running from his mouth and nose, looked up and saw Marlee standing there. "Go back to bed, pumpkin," he said as calmly as if she'd interrupted him making a sandwich. "Everything's all right."

When Marlee was ten, a stranger with a gun had come to their house. He'd held Marlee and her mother hostage in their kitchen for twelve hours, waiting for her father to come home and pay some money the man was owed. Marlee's mother cooked dinner for the stranger and slipped something in the food that made him sick, so that he finally left them alone.

Marlee had both worshipped her father and feared him. In rare peaceful interludes she idolized him. But Frank knew too many dangerous people, and lived a dangerous life that couldn't help but touch her.

And yet, her mother had stayed with him, visiting him faithfully when he was in prison, celebrating when he returned home.

"Why don't you divorce him?" a thirteen-year-old Marlee had asked after her father had landed in jail yet again. "How can you stand to live this way?"

"He's my husband," her mother had said, as if this explained everything. "I love him."

"How can you love a man who's never there for you? Who's never there for *us?*" *How can you love him when he always hurts us?* she wanted to shout. *How can you love him more than you love me?*

"Love is complicated," her mother had answered. "One day you'll understand."

But Marlee had never understood. She'd sworn she wouldn't end up like her mother. She wouldn't fall in love with a man who put his own impulses and crazy dreams ahead of his family. She wouldn't marry a man who broke the law.

Most of all, she would protect her child from pain and disappointment, the way her mother had never protected her.

THE MORE TIME he spent with Marlee and Greg, the more Troy wanted to be with them. Sharing a meal with them, even something as simple as a casual pizza dinner, had given him a glimpse of what it would be like if they were a real family. But before that could ever happen he had to fight Marlee's resistance and get to know his son.

Wednesday, as he cleaned parts, tuned engines or swept the garage bays, he thought about Marlee. She was still beautiful, but he'd noticed differences in her, changes it hurt to see, because he knew he was largely responsible. She was more cautious now, less trusting than the girl he'd known. Though she'd always been independent, now she wore her autonomy like armor.

While he'd spent his time in prison planning how he'd make up for the way he'd hurt her, she'd built a good life for herself and their son.

She'd convinced herself she didn't need him anymore, but she was wrong. Greg needed a father and Marlee deserved a man who loved her. Troy knew no one could fill those roles better than him.

Marlee had done her best to make a home out of the rental house, hanging up frilly curtains and setting out vases of silk flowers. But she deserved real flowers and windows without cracks.

When they'd decided to get married, Troy had promised her a different kind of life than the one she'd had growing up. He hadn't known what that life would look like, but he'd known it would be good. They were in love and everything would work out.

That vision of a perfect life had been naive, but

he had a more definite plan now. The first step was to build a real relationship with his son. Step two: save the down payment for a nicer house. He'd already opened an account. Step three: start a college fund. Marlee would never have to worry about anything again.

He could make it all happen, if Marlee would only give him the chance.

"Is that starter ready for Mr. Childers's bike?" Troy's boss, Wiley Spencer, approached Troy's work bench. A burly man with a head of thick, silver hair and a U.S. Marine Corps tattoo, Wiley kept a thick Bible on one corner of his desk, and pictures of his many grandchildren on the other. There was a rumor that he'd done time for manslaughter a couple of decades earlier, but no one knew for sure.

"Got it right here," Troy said, and lifted the cleaned and rebuilt part from the back of the bench.

Wiley turned the starter over in his hand and nodded. "Looks great." His eyes met Troy's with the kind of gaze that saw right into a man and dared him to lie. "Everything going okay?"

"Yeah. It's going well." Work was good, anyway. He was skilled at his job, and enjoyed learning the intricacies of the newer engines and restoring the older ones.

"What do you do after work?" Wiley asked.

Troy hadn't expected that question. What did Wiley care what he did after work? "Not much," he said. "Go home. Maybe see a friend." He didn't know if he could call Marlee a friend yet, but he was working toward it.

Wiley frowned. "Nobody you met inside, I hope."

"No. This is someone I knew before."

"Guys hang out with the same crowd that got them into trouble before, they end up in trouble again," Wiley said. "You've got a new life now—you have to break all ties with the old one."

"I don't want anything to do with that old life." He had no intention of losing his son a second time. "I'm staying out of trouble."

"Good. When do you see your parole officer?"

"This afternoon. When I'm done here." Every Wednesday afternoon he met with Bernie Martinez. The brief check-in was supposed to help him in his transition to freedom, and to make sure he was keeping his nose clean.

"Don't let me hear of you missing an appointment," Wiley said. "I like to give guys a chance, but you only get one."

"You don't have to worry about me," Troy said. He'd been young and stupid when he'd let himself get involved in his cousin's robbery scheme. He hadn't asked enough questions, and had ignored all signs of trouble. He'd told himself he was trying to provide for Marlee, but he could admit now that he'd wanted to impress her, to build himself up in her eyes by presenting her with money for the baby. To show her he could take care of them. Instead, he'd destroyed everything. Now she thought he was just like her father.

Troy had known men like Frank Britton inside— career criminals who grew so used to prison that they couldn't function outside. Some of those guys were real hard cases, dangerous even, but a lot of them were just sad old men waiting to die.

Troy couldn't imagine ending up like them. He and Frank were nothing alike, no matter what Marlee thought. For most of the people he'd met since his release, one ex-con was the same as any other. It didn't matter to them that he'd been a stupid kid who had exactly one offense on his record, or that he'd been a model prisoner. Most people weren't inclined to give him a second chance, but he hoped he could convince Marlee he deserved one.

After work, he washed as much of the grease from his hands as he could and rode his motorcycle to the low-slung concrete-and-glass building where Bernie had his office.

"Job going okay, finances okay?" Bernie asked after a perfunctory greeting. A stocky man with a neat mustache and thinning hair, Bernie had the weary air of a career bureaucrat.

"Yeah, I'm doing all right," Troy said. "I told you, I'm never going back inside."

"That's good. That kind of determination is important. It's good, too, to realize why you ended up in prison in the first place."

"I ended up in prison because I was stupid enough to trust my cousin. I should have known he was up to something."

"Yes." Bernie nodded thoughtfully. "But you also acted impulsively, without thinking about the consequences. That's a proven recipe for trouble."

"Yeah, I guess so." Troy could have argued that he *had* been thinking the night he decided to go with his cousin—not about what Raymond might be up to, but about what the extra money would mean to Marlee and the baby.

"Is there anything else I can do for you?" Bernie asked.

"Maybe." Troy shifted in his chair. "Do you know an older con from around here, Frank Britton?" The pain in Marlee's voice when she spoke of her father had stayed with him. Maybe Marlee would appreciate it if he could reassure her Frank was still behind bars, or far away, where he would never be able to hurt her again.

"I do. Why?"

"His daughter wants to know how he's doing," Troy lied.

Bernie narrowed his eyes. "I didn't know Frank had a daughter."

"They've lost touch."

Bernie continued to look doubtful. "You tell her Frank's okay. He's stayed out of trouble for four or five years now. I haven't seen him in a while, but I'd have heard if anything happened to him."

"Is he still here? In Austin?" If Frank hadn't tried to get in touch with Marlee after all this time, maybe that was a good sign.

"Last I heard, he was." Bernie shook his head. "Don't bother looking him up. You're making a fresh start, getting your life back in order. Why would you want to go messing around with a career con like Frank?"

"I don't want to see him." He only wanted to know Frank wouldn't be bothering Marlee. Troy could protect her from that, even if she hadn't asked him to.

Bernie made a mark on a piece of paper and closed the file folder on the desk in front of him. "See you next week."

"Yeah." Troy left the building, pausing on the steps to take a deep breath of the warm spring air. The aroma of fresh-cut grass washed over him. Marlee's grass would need cutting soon. He'd take care of it for her. She'd object, but he'd ignore her. Now that he was free, he intended to do all the things he hadn't been able to before. He would show Marlee he'd earned her forgiveness and trust.

MARLEE FELT a flutter of apprehension as she watched from the front window as Troy backed a pickup truck into her driveway Saturday morning. When he'd called to say he was bringing a surprise, she hadn't expected the two large cartons that filled the bed of the truck. Even from here she could read the lettering that proclaimed Heavy-duty Washer and Electric Dryer.

He cut the engine and climbed out of the cab, his long legs quickly covering the distance to the rear of the truck. Marlee met him as he was lowering the tailgate, Greg running ahead. "What do you think you're doing?" she asked.

"I'm bringing you your surprise." He grinned. "What do you think?"

"I think you should drive right back to the store and see if they'll give you a refund."

Troy climbed into the bed of the pickup and started unloading a dolly. "Nope. I'm installing these right now."

"No, you aren't."

"But, Mom! We won't have to go to the Laundromat." Greg hung over the side of the truck and watched Troy maneuver the dolly under the carton for the washer.

Troy smiled at the boy. "When I'm ready to hook these up, I'll let you help."

"All right!"

"You're not going to be hooking up anything," Marlee said. "I can't accept a gift like this." *Not from you,* she added silently.

He leaned on the dolly and sighed in exasperation. "Why not?"

She folded her arms across her chest. "I don't want you to think you can buy your way into my good graces."

He leaned closer to her and lowered his voice so that only she could hear. "You think I'm trying to seduce you with appliances? Believe me, I could do better than that." The heat in his gaze confirmed he had the power to seduce her with more than gifts and gestures. She remembered how close she had come to giving in to her desire for him the other night up on the bluff. She'd spent seven years trying to forget the way his touch, his kiss, the very brush of his skin against her own could make her feel, and within hours of seeing him again, it had all come rushing back.

She hugged her arms tighter across her chest and strengthened her resolve. "I don't want to owe you anything," she said.

Troy set the dolly upright and planted both hands on the washer box, leaning toward her and speaking quietly. "You've got it wrong, Marlee. *I'm* the one who owes *you*. I should've been supporting you all these years and I haven't been. This is just payback."

She worried her lower lip between her teeth. "Greg and I are fine without you. I don't need—"

"Then don't think of this as a gift to you—think of it as something for Greg. He hates going to the Laundromat, right?" He raised his voice on the last sentence so the boy could hear.

"Right!" Greg said.

Troy grabbed the handles of the dolly and tilted it back once more, biceps bunching with the effort. "Now, come on. Let me in. I have to return the truck tonight."

His voice was calm, but his expression dared her to defy him. Reluctantly, she stepped out of the way. She couldn't deny she'd longed for a washer and dryer of her own. As Greg's father, she guessed Troy should contribute to his support. But she was determined not to rely on Troy for anything. Hadn't he proved years ago that he was undependable?

She retreated to the bathroom while he and Greg installed the new appliances. She spent the next hour scouring tile and polishing mirrors, humming to herself to drown out the low rumble of Troy's voice, followed by Greg's higher-pitched one. The sound was foreign to this house, her sanctuary no man had ever invaded. Yet it didn't seem out of place, more like bass notes adding the underpinning to a melody.

Part of her enjoyed having Troy here. She liked having someone take care of things for her. Admitting it made her feel weak, and she despised the weakness. She'd worked so hard to prove she didn't need a man. Hadn't she done just fine as a girl, without her father around? When she'd met Troy she'd been strong and independent, not afraid of anything, out for a little fun.

Then she'd made the mistake of falling in love, of allowing herself to depend on someone else. Look how that had turned out.

Sure, being alone was hard sometimes. But it was better than letting down her guard and giving another person the power to hurt her again.

After a while, she noticed she could no longer hear Troy or Greg. She went to the kitchen to check on them. It was empty, though a toolbox sat open on the table. A draft chilled her and she saw the window over the sink was open. When she looked out, Troy was bent over the picnic table, Greg at his side.

"What are you two doing out there?" she called.

Troy raised his head, then nodded to the piece of glass he'd been cutting. "I'm fixing that broken windowpane. Greg's helping."

Marlee frowned, struggling with whether to thank him or protest. "You didn't have to go to all that trouble," she said. "The landlord will take care of it."

"Then why hasn't he?"

Because Marlee would rather maintain her privacy than have her landlord poking around in her life. A cracked windowpane was a small inconvenience compared to the peace of being left alone.

Her landlord was a recent arrival in Austin, and knew nothing of her family history. Many of her neighbors were newcomers, too. No one paid much attention to her, and that was how she liked it. "It was fine the way it was," she said.

"No, it wasn't."

Troy turned back to his work, and began to explain to Greg how the rotary glass cutter operated. Marlee watched her son, who often had trouble sitting still long enough to finish his supper, stand motionless beside Troy, hanging on his every word. No one else had ever made such an impression on him. Was some instinct drawing him to his father?

Not wanting to think about such things, she retreated to her bedroom with a book. A little while later, Greg found her. "Can Troy stay for supper?" he asked.

She laid aside her book and looked at her son. He was growing up so fast. Already he was losing the babyish softness in his face, and he'd grown at least an inch in the past month. Every change seemed to make him resemble Troy more, and her less. "Maybe Troy doesn't want to stay for supper," she said.

"I already asked him. I think he wants to stay, but he said I had to check with you."

Troy had been with them the whole day already, rubbing her nerves raw, intruding on her neatly ordered life. "I don't know, honey—"

"Please, Mom."

How could she say no to that heartfelt plea? "All right." She sighed. "I'll thaw more pork chops."

Greg ran off to deliver the good news. A few minutes later, Troy stood just outside her room. "Greg invited me to supper," he said. "Are you sure it's all right?"

His shoulders filled the narrow doorway, his head coming to within only a few inches of the top. Marlee sat up, self-conscious of reclining on her bed in front of this man who reminded her too well of what else could be done in a bed. "Of course it's all right," she said, surprised at how calm she sounded, despite the fiery emotions raging within her.

"I have to return the truck, but I can be back in about an hour."

She nodded. "Sure. Dinner should be ready by then."

He hesitated, his gaze lingering on her. She sat absolutely still on the bed, listening to the throb of her pulse. He stared at her for what seemed like a long time, his dark eyes smoldering in a face that was otherwise stony. Only those burning eyes and the white knuckles of his hand gripping the door frame betrayed the depth of his emotions. Then, in a sudden, explosive movement he shoved himself away and left.

Marlee collapsed against the pillows, weak with longing, angry at herself for feeling this way. She'd thought cutting contact with him all those years ago would destroy any hold he had over her. Apparently, the physical connection they'd once shared was stronger than she'd imagined. The more she was around Troy, the more those old feelings tried to assert themselves.

But her mind was surely more powerful than her body. And she knew that temporary sexual satisfaction wouldn't make up for the independent future she'd have to surrender to be with Troy. Her whole world revolved around him when she was nineteen. Watching him being sent to prison had devastated her. She'd vowed never to be that emotionally dependent on anyone again. She was strong and self-sufficient, but she sensed that Troy had the power to make her break that promise.

CHAPTER FIVE

TROY STOPPED at a convenience store on his way back to Marlee's. It didn't seem right to show up for dinner without something to contribute, so he chose a half-gallon of ice cream from the freezer. At the counter, he picked up the newspaper. He'd check the movie listings and if anything good was playing, maybe he could talk Marlee and Greg into coming with him to a show.

He wanted an excuse to prolong their time together. All afternoon, even as he reveled in the time spent with his son, he'd been aware of Marlee's presence. Her perfume lingered in rooms even after she'd left. The sound of her singing drifted to him as he worked. When he'd walked into her bedroom and seen her lying against the pillows, desire tore at him. He'd summoned every ounce of self-control to keep from acting on it.

Outside the store, he stowed the ice cream in his saddlebags and flipped through the paper. But before he got to the theater listings, an article caught his attention. Manager Saves Woman From Fire, the headline read. The story was accompanied by a picture of a silver-haired man next to the remains of a burned building. Something about the man was familiar. Troy's gaze flickered to the caption below the picture. Frank Britton, manager at the Lakeside Apartments, rescued Alma Edwards from her burning home Thursday night.

Movies forgotten, Troy quickly read the rest of the story, then stuffed the paper in the saddlebag with the ice cream. Marlee would want to see this.

Greg answered the door, greeting Troy with a bear hug that made Troy feel ten feet tall. How could one little boy inspire so much joy? "Hope you like ice cream," Troy said.

"I *love* ice cream."

Troy pulled the carton from behind his back. "How does mint chocolate chip sound?"

"Awesome."

Troy chuckled. "Let's go show your mom."

Marlee was in the kitchen, frying pork chops. Troy paused in the doorway to enjoy a lingering look at her shapely legs.

She must have heard him come in because she looked over her shoulder at him. "What are you staring at?" she demanded.

He grinned. As if she didn't know. "I brought some ice cream," he said, holding up the carton.

"Oh. Thanks. Better put it in the freezer." She turned to her son. "Greg, set the table for me, please."

Greg hurried to a low cabinet and began pulling out plates. "Remember, the forks go on the left, knives and spoons on the right," Marlee said.

"Mom! I know!"

She rolled her eyes at Troy and he smiled at the shared joke. He walked over to the stove and pulled the article he'd torn out of the newspaper from his back pocket. "I brought something to show you," he said, his voice low so Greg wouldn't hear him.

Marlee paused, spatula in hand. "What is it?"

He pointed to the photo. "This article. It's about your dad."

She stiffened, and her face lost all color. He waited while she read the article, which told the story of her father's unexpected heroism, risking his life to save his elderly tenant.

"That is your father, isn't it?" Troy asked.

She shrugged and threw the paper on the counter. "So?"

"So now you know where he is."

"Too close for comfort."

He glanced through the doorway to her small dining room at Greg. The boy was busy arranging silverware beside each plate. "You don't think he'd hurt you, do you?" Maybe she knew something about Frank that Troy didn't.

"No, of course not!" She took a deep breath and spoke in a softer voice. "He'd never physically hurt me, but I still don't have any interest in seeing him. I don't want to talk about it." She moved the frying pan off the burner and began putting the pork chops on a plate.

Troy wished he could read Marlee's mind and know what she was thinking. She had never really talked about her father; she'd told him once that her father hadn't been around much when she was growing up because he was either in prison or hiding from the law. Did she think Troy—who'd made one mistake and knew exactly what it had cost him—would end up like her father? Did she believe he, too, would abandon her and Greg again, lured by a life that her father hadn't been able to resist?

I'm not like that, he wanted to tell her.

But words meant nothing unless backed up by action.

MARLEE WENT THROUGH the motions of setting dinner on the table, but her mind was focused on the newspaper article Troy had shown her. Seeing her father's picture after all these years had been a shock. He'd looked older, of course, but the thick hair and piercing gaze were the same as she remembered. He'd always been so handsome...

She shook her head. What did appearances matter when the man himself was anything but handsome? She'd sworn long ago never to have anything to do with her father again. The past was just that—the past. Better to leave it alone.

"Dinner's ready," she announced, taking her place at the table.

Greg said grace, and she began passing plates. Troy helped himself to pork chops, mashed potatoes, green beans and rolls. "This is delicious," he said after a few bites.

Marlee smiled, flattered in spite of herself. "You act as if you haven't eaten in a month of Sundays," she teased.

"It's been a long time since I've had a meal this good," he said. His eyes caught and held hers. "It's been a long time since I've enjoyed a lot of things."

She looked away, the tension between them returning tenfold.

"I like it when Troy comes over, don't you, Mom?" Greg grinned at each of them in turn.

"It's very nice," Marlee murmured, afraid of showing too much enthusiasm. She didn't want Troy to get the wrong idea. He was here as Greg's father, not because he meant anything to her.

"Can Troy come to my open house?" Greg asked.

She blinked, caught off guard. "Greg, I don't know…"

"What open house?" Troy asked.

"Next week, at my school," Greg said. "It's like a party. We're doing special projects and artwork and we'll have refreshments."

"It's really just for parents," Marlee said. She bit her lip as she caught her mistake. Troy *was* Greg's father, even though they hadn't publicly acknowledged it. How long would he be willing to go along with keeping the secret?

"Friends can come, too. Mrs. Ramirez said," Greg announced.

"Then I think I should come," Troy said pointedly.

Marlee nodded. "Yes, of course."

"My friend Rachel Minor lost a tooth at school last week," Greg said. "She was showing me it was loose, wiggling it back and forth, and all of a sudden it just came out. There was blood and everything. It fell in the sand under the swings and when we found it, it had all this dirt sticking to it, and blood and everything."

"That's horrible," Marlee said.

"No, it's cool." Troy grinned, and Greg grinned back, two members of that male club that thought blood and dirt were excellent topics of dinner-table conversation.

Regret and more than a little guilt pinched her as she watched father and son together. *This* was why Greg needed a man in his life, for this kind of understanding and acceptance.

Fear had made her cautious where Greg was concerned, fear that he'd be hurt by a man who swept in and out of their lives, the way her father had done. But was she protecting Greg—or merely being selfish, keeping her boy to herself? Maybe his need for male guidance outweighed her fears.

The open house would be a good first step. They'd see where they stood from there.

After dinner, Troy insisted on helping Marlee clear the table. He followed her to the kitchen and stacked the dishes in the sink. "I meant to fix that hinge this afternoon," he said, frowning at the broken cabinet door. "Let me get a screwdriver. It'll only take a minute."

While Troy tackled the hinge, Marlee returned to the dining room, where she cornered Greg. "Time to do your homework, young man," she said.

"Mo-om! I don't have school until Monday."

"That's no reason to put things off until the last minute." She picked up his spelling book from a chair by the door and opened it on the table. "Let me help you learn these spelling words."

Greg slumped in a chair and tapped out a rhythm on the table with his pencil. "I want Troy to help me," he said.

"Did somebody say my name?" Troy stepped into the room, wiping his hands on a dish towel.

Greg grinned up at him. "Help me learn these spelling words, Troy."

"Sure thing, bud."

"Did you fix the hinge already?" she asked.

"Yup. It only needed a new screw."

"Okay, I'll go do the dishes."

Marlee shoved back her chair and fled to the kitchen, not wanting Greg to see she was upset. Oh, it hurt to see her little boy choose a man who was practically a stranger over her!

Don't be silly, it's just homework, she told herself. She squirted detergent over the dishes in the sink and began running water, drowning out the sound of voices from the other room.

She was washing the last pan when Troy returned to the kitchen. "He's a really smart kid," he said.

She nodded, scrubbing at the side of the pot harder than necessary.

A firm hand gripped her shoulder and she looked up into Troy's understanding eyes. "You're still his mom," he said. "Nobody will ever take your place. Don't think I'm trying to."

She plunged her hands into the soapy water. "You don't have to apologize. Of course he's fascinated with you. He's never been around many men before. I guess I should have dated more, or enrolled him in Big Brothers, or—"

"Hey, relax, you've done a great job. He's a terrific kid." He squeezed her shoulder. "I'm proud of you both."

Marlee wanted to tell him she didn't need his praise, but the warm feeling it gave her inside proved how wrong she was. Since her mother's death, she'd had no one to reassure her she was making the right choices for her son, no one to confirm that he *was* turning out well. To hear Troy praise her when he could just as easily have judged her harshly made her ridiculously happy and relieved.

On the heels of these emotions came the physical awareness of his hand, heavy on her shoulder, his body close to hers. His warmth seeped into her. Having Troy back in her life—even though she kept him at a distance—reminded her of how *alone* she'd been for too long.

She closed her eyes, trying to regain her composure. But he must have mistaken it for a gesture of invitation, and he covered her lips with his.

The kiss was gentle, tentative even. He stilled, waiting for her to take the lead. She put her hand up to push him away, but as she rested her palm against his chest, she was distracted by the wonderful, solid feel of him. Troy was the man who'd taught her all about kissing, who'd shown her how magical the connection between a man and a woman could be.

The chance to relive those memories seduced her, and she leaned into his embrace,

She opened her mouth and heat burned through her, melting her inhibitions, dissolving her fears. The passion she'd thought dead and gone flared to life once more.

A low moan vibrated and Marlee couldn't tell if it came from her or from Troy. He pressed his body against her, his desire evident. She tore her lips from his, and let her head fall back.

He trailed hot kisses along her throat, licking and suckling until she thought she'd go mad. Her nipples strained against his chest. When he brought his hand up to fondle her, she stifled a cry of pleasure.

"Tro-oy! How do you say this word?"

Greg's call clanged like an alarm bell in her head. Gasping, she struggled to free herself from Troy's arms, and from the sensual spell he'd cast on her. He groaned, and reluctantly relinquished his hold on her. "I guess I'd better go."

She nodded, still too breathless to speak. When he was gone, she sagged against the counter. What had she done, letting Troy kiss her like that? What if Greg had walked in?

Or worse, what if Greg hadn't interrupted them when he did? She could have lost herself with a man she hardly knew, despite all that had happened in the past.

She'd been a fool to take that kind of chance. She immersed her shaking hands in the dishwater and began scrubbing the pan again.

Prison changed people—how could it not? Troy was more serious than he'd been before, but what else was different? Had he become violent behind bars? More inclined to make his own rules, regardless of what society dictated?

Yet the man who had held her just now—who'd listened to her son and helped him with his homework—didn't strike her as violent or disorderly. If anything, Troy was gentler than she remembered, the brashness of youth replaced by a more thoughtful kindness.

At the same time, there was a seriousness to him she didn't remember—an intensity that both frightened and attracted her. He was, as Trish had said, the kind of man who could hold his own if things got rough.

But she'd already come through plenty of rough times without his help. She'd allow him to be a part of her life for Greg's sake, but she certainly wouldn't let herself *need* him.

TROY SAT across from Greg at the dining-room table, buzzing with the adrenaline in his veins. Just as well he and Marlee had been interrupted. Troy needed time to cool off. He'd never meant for the situation to get so out of hand, but he'd looked at Marlee's upturned face, her eyes closed, lips slightly parted, and he'd seen, not the woman who'd rejected him and thrown away his letters, but the girl he'd loved with all his being.

No matter what she said, that kiss told him Marlee

still felt something for him. Physically, at least, though whether there was anything beyond lust, he couldn't tell.

"What does this say?" Greg turned the school-book toward him and pointed to a word.

"Because," Troy read.

"*B-E-C-A-U-S-E*." Greg sounded out each letter. "Because."

"Try this one." Troy pointed to the next word on the list.

"I know that one. It's ready—*R-E-A-D-Y*."

"That's great." Troy listened as Greg completed the rest of the words on his worksheet. His son deserved his full attention, but he couldn't tear his thoughts away from the woman in the kitchen.

What did it say about him that he refused to take no for an answer? After the first few months, when Marlee didn't answer his letters from prison, he'd figured out she didn't intend to. He'd been hurt and angry, but he kept writing anyway, alternately pouring his fury and his love for her onto the paper. Yes, she'd refused to stand by him, but he knew how much it had cost her to go with him even as far as she had—to visit him in jail and sit through the trial. The District Attorney's case against him had sounded horrible even to his ears— how much worse must it have seemed to a girl who'd been disappointed time after time by her father's pro-testations of innocence? As much as Troy raged against her refusal to believe him, part of him understood why she couldn't, and that understanding kept him writing.

That, and hope for their child.

He got through the toughest days of his confinement by imagining their child. When he left prison, he hadn't even known if the baby would be a boy or girl. They hadn't picked out names.

As her due date neared, then passed with still no word, he'd resorted to calling his mother and begging her for some news of the child.

And now here he was, trying to build those fantasies and longings into what? A family—the three of them together, as they were meant to be.

BY THE TIME she finished the dishes, Marlee had regained her composure. She dried her hands, smoothed her hair, then went into the dining room. "Time to get ready for bed, Greg. Say good-night to Troy."

"Aw, Mom."

"Good night, Greg. I'll see you soon." Troy tousled the boy's hair and Greg threw his arms around him in a surprisingly strong hug.

"Go on, now," Marlee said. "I'll be there in a minute."

Reluctantly, Greg shuffled out of the room.

Troy stared after his son. "I used to try to picture what he'd be like," he said. "But the reality is a lot better than anything I could have imagined."

She had a sudden vision of him, alone in a prison cell, thinking of the son he never knew. "I thought you'd forget about us."

"Never. But I guess you tried hard to forget about me. Isn't that why you didn't answer my letters?"

"I thought a clean break would be better." She met his gaze, finding courage by reminding herself of all the reasons she'd turned her back on him after his conviction. "I grew up with a con for a father. I wasn't about to put my child through that kind of hell."

"I'm not your father," he said. "I made a stupid mistake and ended up in the wrong place at the wrong time, but I'm not going to do it again."

He sounded so positive. For Greg's sake, she wanted to believe him. "Maybe you won't. But what you've done will stay with you the rest of your life. And if people find out, it brands Greg, too. When I was a child, my classmates talked about my father as if he was a monster. They'd see his picture in the paper when he was arrested, and couldn't wait to tell me all about it. Parents didn't want their sons and daughters associating with me, and teachers suspected me whenever anything disappeared from their desks or from classmates' lockers. I couldn't bear it if Greg had to go through any of that."

"Of course you couldn't. I couldn't either. But again, I'm not your father. My arrest was years ago. It scarcely made the papers. Besides, none of Greg's classmates were even born when it happened. There's no reason it should ever come up again. Trust me."

Did he know what he was asking? Marlee hadn't trusted anyone in a long time. "Good night, Troy."

"I'll see you Monday, then. At Greg's open house."

"Right." She followed him to the door, and locked it behind him. Then she stood at the window, watching through the blinds as he mounted the motorcycle and sped into the darkness. Only then did she walk down the hall to Greg's room.

"Why aren't you ready for bed?" she asked. He was supposed to be in his pajamas already; instead, he sprawled in the middle of the floor, racing a plastic motorcycle over the hills and valleys of the bunched-up rug beside his bed.

"I wanted to play with my motorcycle first," he said. A gift from Troy, the motorcycle had become Greg's most prized possession. He sat up. "Do you think Troy will take me riding on his motorcycle soon?"

"You have to be much older to ride a motorcycle," Marlee told him.

"How much older?"

"All grown up. Come on. As long as you're still awake, I think you need a bath."

"Mo-om!"

"No arguing. Into the bathroom with you." Bath time had been her favorite ritual when Greg was a baby. Sheltered in the little bathroom with the warm water and steamed-up mirror, listening to her child giggle as he played with bubbles, Marlee had felt far removed from the problems of her past or worries about the future. She could use a little of that comfort now, she thought as she ran Greg's bathwater.

"I really like Troy," Greg said as he stood first on one foot, then the other beside the tub, peeling off his socks.

"And he really likes you." She took a towel and washcloth from the cabinet over the toilet and laid them on the edge of the sink. "Do you want bubbles?" She picked up the pink bottle of bubble bath from the edge of the tub.

"Bubbles are for girls."

She stared at him. "But I thought you liked them."

He pulled his shirt over his head. "I just think maybe I'm a little too old for that."

"All right." Marlee replaced the bottle and checked the temperature of the water while Greg finished undressing.

"You like Troy, don't you, Mom?" Greg asked as he stepped into the water.

"Well, I... Yes, I like Troy." She found it difficult not to like him, considering how sorry he seemed to be for the pain he'd caused her. But liking him and allowing him to be a part of Greg's life didn't mean they could ever go back to the intimate relationship they'd had before Troy was arrested. She'd been too willing to give someone else the responsibility for her happiness then, but she knew better now.

"Troy says I'm a good speller," Greg said as he rubbed soap onto a washcloth.

"You are. Don't forget to wash your elbows and knees."

"I only missed one word and he said it was a hard one."

"What's the word?"

"Pen. The kind you write with? It sounds like it should have an *I* in it, but it doesn't. It's an *E*."

"But now you remember that, and you'll spell it right next time."

"That's what Troy said. He said we should always learn from our mistakes."

Had Troy learned from his mistakes? She hoped so. Greg deserved a father he could look up to.

"I'm glad Troy's coming to my open house," Greg said. "I want to show him my class and where I sit. And he can meet my teacher."

She had never known Greg to be this excited about anyone. "Greg, honey, you've only known Troy a few days," she said. "What makes him so cool?"

Greg shrugged. "I don't know. He just…he really likes me. He treats me like I'm special."

"Oh, honey, you *are* special." She leaned over to hug him.

He squirmed out of her embrace. "You have to say that 'cause you're my mom. But Troy thought I was special right away."

"How do you know that, honey?"

"Because of the way he looked at me."

She felt a catch in her chest. She knew that look.

She'd seen it again this evening in the kitchen, a look Troy had given her when they were young and in love. But she must have been wrong—there was too much hurt between them now to leave any room for love.

"Hurry up," she urged Greg. "Time for bed." She checked to make sure he'd washed thoroughly, then helped him out of the tub and into pajamas. After reading a chapter of *How to Eat Fried Worms* she tucked him in and kissed him good-night.

Restless, she went into the kitchen to make a cup of tea. But when she flipped on the light, the first thing she saw was the newspaper clipping Troy had brought, the story about her dad.

She sat at the table and read the article again, then her gaze returned to the photograph. When she was a little girl, she didn't understand why her father was away so much. When he was gone she would sometimes take the wedding photograph of her parents off the hall table and sleep with it beside her. Her mother, in a white gown and veil, smiled at her father, who looked out at the viewer, black eyes sparkling, hair slicked back, grinning like a movie star.

Age and hard times had stolen those looks. At some point, his nose had been broken and not set properly. He wasn't smiling in the newspaper photo, and deep lines were etched into his face. But his eyes were the same, dark and alert, with a glint as if he knew a great secret.

Her fingers crumpled the paper. The neighborhood where the fire had occurred was only a few miles from here. Her father was that close.

When she'd thought about him at all, she'd assumed he was still in prison, locked up in Huntsville where he couldn't hurt her or anyone else. How long had he been out?

She pushed the paper away. It didn't matter. Her father wasn't part of her life anymore. She wouldn't put herself—or Greg—through the pain of being close to someone they couldn't depend on.

Was she taking the same risk with Troy? She

knew there would always be a chance he'd go back to his old ways. Even so, she had a hard time thinking of him as a hardened criminal.

He'd been gentle with her. How had he understood so instinctively what she'd been feeling when Greg asked him for help instead of her?

Could she fall in love with Troy all over again? Her feelings for him before had been so intense, her hurt when he left so great...

No! She was past feeling anything for Troy but casual friendship. The kiss they'd shared this afternoon had been a mistake, a combination of nearness and memories that were best not revisited.

Marlee took a deep, steadying breath. All right, she'd acknowledged her physical weakness for Troy. Now she would just have to guard against it. Given enough practice, and enough time, she could conquer her desires in order to protect herself and her son.

CHAPTER SIX

THE HALLS OF Waterloo Elementary School rang with the cries of excited children and the exclamations of proud parents. Everywhere Marlee looked, she saw men squeezed into child-size chairs, smiling mothers studying stick-figure drawings and children beaming as they showed off their work, their desks, their classrooms, their school.

"Hurry up, Mom!" Greg pulled on her hand, a tugboat towing a barge through a sea of people.

She heard the rumble of Troy's chuckle as he walked beside her. "Were we ever this enthusiastic about school?" he asked.

"Maybe in first grade," Marlee said. "I liked school pretty well, at least when I was Greg's age."

"That's because you were smart," he observed.

Greg led them into his classroom. Mrs. Ramirez was speaking to a group of parents at the front of the room. Marlee began a promenade along the chalkboard, searching the drawings and work sheets for Greg's name.

She stopped in front of a spelling test adorned with a gold star. "I'm so proud of you," she told her son and hugged him close. Greg was so smart—already a better student than she'd ever been. He'd be able to do anything he wanted with his future—become a doctor or a lawyer or an engineer. All the sacrifices she made now would be worth it to make sure her son never had to endure the same hardships. One day, when he was much older, she'd tell him about his grandfather and her childhood, so he could see how lucky he really was.

"Hey, look at this." Troy touched her elbow and pointed to a drawing of a stick-figure boy and man on a motorcycle with oversize tires. When Marlee read Greg's handwriting at the bottom of the page—Me and Troy—her chest felt hollow. Greg used to draw pictures of her and him together. Knowing Troy was her son's new favorite subject stung.

"Do you really like it?" Greg asked.

"I really do." Troy cleared his throat. "It's a terrific picture."

"I'll give it to you when we get to take our stuff home." Greg turned to Marlee. "Can I go say hi to Rachel?"

"All right," Marlee said. "But stay in this room."

The boy raced away and she and Troy continued to search the displays for his work.

"Look at that math work sheet." Troy nodded to another of Greg's papers. He leaned closer and spoke in a low, confiding tone. "I can't get over how smart he is. He must get it from you."

She blushed at the compliment. As they reached the end of the chalkboard and turned to take in the papers tacked to the bulletin boards along the side of the room, she became aware of the curious glances they were attracting from other parents. She recognized many of them from previous school gatherings. *They're wondering who Troy is,* she thought. *They want to know who he is to* me.

She'd spent a lot of time contemplating that question this week, but still had no answer. Troy was the first man she'd loved. The father of her child— the only man she'd allowed into her life. But he was also the man who'd betrayed her trust. A reminder of a past she'd tried hard to escape.

Yet her physical attraction to him pulled at her like an undertow—combined with the temptation to let him take care of her, as he seemed to want to do. The responsibilities of raising her son and tending to every detail of their lives weighed heavy. The idea of giving up some of that burden was appealing.

But that was no better reason to start a relationship than some fantasy about true love.

She realized Troy was watching her intently, as if trying to read her thoughts. At one time, he'd known her better, more intimately, than anyone else on earth. But not now. Her thoughts and emotions were her own, not to be shared.

Traffic was backing up behind them, so Troy nudged Marlee's arm and they moved on. "Is my being here going to cause problems for you?" he asked. He must have noticed the curious glances they were getting.

"What kind of problems?"

"Gossip. Rumors?"

"Probably." She'd never been overly friendly with the other parents, but she was sure they'd noticed she always attended these functions alone. "I guess having a few mothers speculate about the good-looking guy I'm with isn't the worst thing that could happen to me," she said. "And Greg's thrilled that you're here."

TROY LOOKED OVER to where Greg and a little girl—his friend Rachel of the missing front tooth—were raiding the refreshment table. The boy had hugged him when Troy arrived at the house, and thanked him for coming. As if anything short of death would have kept him from the event.

He turned back to Marlee, who was still studying him. "So my appearance meets with your approval?" Instead of his motorcycle leathers, he wore khaki slacks and a denim shirt with a Tabasco tie.

"I like the tie," Marlee said.

It was as close to a compliment as she'd come since they'd reconnected. He felt in danger of busting his buttons.

They completed their circuit of the room and stopped to say hello to Mrs. Ramirez. Greg's teacher smiled and extended her hand. "How nice to see you, Ms. Britton." She looked questioningly at Troy.

"This is my friend Troy," Greg said, rejoining them.

"Troy Denton." He shook her hand.

Mrs. Ramirez beamed. "I've heard so much about

you, Mr. Denton," she said. "You've made quite an impression on Greg."

What could he say to that? For all Marlee's aloofness, Greg had taken to Troy immediately, almost as if the little boy sensed there was something special about their relationship.

He respected Marlee's wish to protect Greg from the shock of suddenly learning he had a father, and he understood her reluctance to deal with the uncomfortable questions that would follow. But one day soon he would insist they tell Greg the truth.

"Troy, come meet Sugar and Spice." Greg tugged him toward the cage that held the class guinea pigs. "They're both girls," Greg said. "We had a rabbit that was a boy, but it kept getting out, so it went to live with Rebecca Trovar, who has other rabbits."

"It's good they found a home for him," Troy said. "Do you help take care of Sugar and Spice?"

"Oh, sure. We all take turns. But you have to be real gentle with them, or they get scared." He stroked one finger down Sugar's brown-and-white side through the bars.

Troy felt an overwhelming rush of tenderness. His son was kind and smart. While he had long enjoyed the *idea* of being a father, he hadn't imagined it was possible to feel so connected to a child he had met only a week ago.

Love was like that, he guessed—mysterious and powerful and defying all logic.

WHEN THEY RETURNED home, Greg ran ahead into the house as Troy followed Marlee to the front door. "Thank you for inviting me tonight," he said. "I want to be involved in his life that way. Thank you for understanding."

"You're welcome."

He put his hand on the porch post above her head and leaned toward her. She held her breath, wondering if he would try to kiss her and if she'd be able to pull away.

Instead, he straightened and took a step back. "I'll call you tomorrow," he said.

Marlee watched him walk away, waiting to feel the relief she expected, but instead she was confused. She still didn't know where Troy fit in her life, or what role she wanted him to play. Right now, he was a friend interested in Greg, but how long could he be just that? If she told Greg the truth, would Troy become an even bigger part of their lives? Would he insist on having more of a say in Greg's future? Could she handle that?

Greg came out of the house, slipped under her arm and hugged her. "Tonight was fun," he said.

"It was. I'm very proud of you." She smoothed his hair. "You know that, don't you?"

"Yeah." He was silent a moment, then said, "Do you think Troy is proud of me, too?"

Troy again. "I'm sure he is," she said. "He commented on how smart you are."

"He liked the motorcycle I drew, too."

"I love you, honey."

"I love you, too, Mom. It was a good night, wasn't it?" he repeated.

"Yes, it was." Good if only because Greg was pleased. That was all she wanted—to give her son a safe, stable childhood filled with happy memories— the kind she hadn't known.

If that meant finding a place for Troy in their little circle, then she would do it. But she wouldn't let down her guard around him. If he did anything to upset her son or threaten his happiness, she would fight him with everything she had.

IT WAS STILL EARLY when Troy returned to his apartment, barely eight o'clock. He parked the bike and started up the stairs to his unit, then froze at the sight of a dark figure in the doorway.

"Hey, Troy." His parole office, Bernie Martinez, stepped into the light.

Troy moved warily up the steps. "Hey," he said. He didn't bother to ask what Bernie was doing here. As a parolee, Troy was subject to visits by Bernie or other officers of the law at any time. They could search his apartment, test his blood or urine or saliva or question his friends. For the duration of his parole, he was still considered a prisoner of the state, with only limited freedom.

He couldn't wait until he was no longer confined by such restrictions—when he wouldn't have the constant reminder of his time in prison. He wanted to put that behind him, but for the next year or two, he was still a convict, and not to be trusted.

"I was on my way home and thought I'd stop and see how you're doing," Bernie said.

"Sure." Troy unlocked the door of his apartment. "Come on in."

He led the way into the small, sparsely furnished front room. He hadn't bought much, just a sagging recliner, a coffee table with a radio and a stack of books piled on it. Bernie looked around. "No TV? What do you do in the evenings?"

"I listen to the radio or read." He dropped his keys onto the counter that jutted out from the kitchen. "Can I get you something to drink? A soda or a glass of water?"

"No, thanks." Bernie shoved his hands in his pockets and followed Troy into the kitchen. "How's the job going?"

"It's okay."

"You making friends on the outside?"

Troy had spent every free minute with Marlee and Greg. They were his priorities now. "I'm all right, Bernie." He took a can of Coke from the refrigerator and opened it.

"It's important to establish ties to the community," Bernie said. "Relationships that don't have anything to do with prison."

"I'm doing all right," he said again, his voice sharper.

Bernie frowned. "Did you ever get in touch with Frank Britton?"

Troy hadn't even thought about Frank since the night he'd shown Marlee the story in the paper. "No.

I saw an article about him in the paper, though. He saved a woman from a fire."

"Yes. Imagine that. Frank a hero."

Troy nodded. The Frank Marlee had described looked out only for himself. But people could change. Troy knew that better than anyone.

"What about your cousin, Raymond?" Bernie asked. "You ever hear from him?"

He set the soda can down hard on the counter, some of the Coke sloshing over his knuckles. "No. I haven't spoken to him since we were arrested." And never would. He hated being reminded of the man who'd brought him so much trouble.

"He just got out. Part of that big push to relieve prison overcrowding. I thought he might be in touch."

"If he knows what's good for him, he won't be."

Bernie looked around the empty apartment again. "Who do you hang out with?" he asked.

"What do you mean?"

"Who are your friends?"

"I don't have time for a lot of socializing."

"What about family? Do any of them live in the area?"

Marlee and Greg were his family now, but that bond felt new and fragile. He hated to make them a part of this ugly side of his life.

"I'm not asking just to be nosy," Bernie said. "It's important for you to have a support group. Parolees who have friends and family they can rely on are less likely to return to prison."

His father had been dead for years. His brother lived on the other side of the country and they rarely spoke. And although Troy saw his mother regularly, they weren't close. The friends he'd had before had moved on with their lives. When Troy went to prison, he'd disappeared from their lives and they from his.

"You don't have to worry about me," he said. "I'm doing okay."

"Where were you tonight?" Bernie asked.

He hesitated, a lie on the tip of his tongue. But hadn't he said he was done with dishonesty? "I was with my son and his mother. Parents' night at his school."

Troy almost smiled at the genuine surprise on Bernie's face. "I didn't know you had a son," he said.

"He was born while I was locked up," Troy said. "I'm just getting to know him. He's a great kid." He wished he had a picture to show Bernie. Why hadn't he asked Marlee for one he could keep in his wallet? Not having a photo reminded him of how tenuous his ties to his son were.

"So you and his mother are close?"

"She's still mad at me for being stupid. She lets me see the boy, but she won't let me tell him I'm his father." He hadn't meant to share this last bit of information, but it felt good to confide in someone.

Bernie shook his head. "That's rough."

"Yeah, well, we're working on it." He took another drink of Coke.

"What if she never tells him the truth?"

"She will." He wouldn't agree to lie much longer. He wouldn't add to his sins by letting Greg think his father couldn't be trusted. His voice grew rough. "I love him."

"So you and his mother stayed in touch while you were in prison. How come you never mentioned her before?"

"I looked her up after I got out. It's a long story."

"I'm in no hurry."

Had Bernie become Troy's therapist as well as his parole officer? Or was this part of the state's efforts to reduce recidivism? In any case, Troy wasn't about to reveal he was carrying a torch for a woman who'd returned every letter he'd sent her. "I don't want to talk about it," he said.

"At least tell me who she is."

"Why?"

"It's my job to know who you're associating with."

One more reminder his life was still not his own. "Her name's Marlee. Marlee Britton. She's Frank's daughter."

Bernie's eyebrows rose, the only sign that this revelation shocked him. "Be careful there," he said. "Frank has powerful friends. They could make trouble for you if you upset his daughter."

Troy didn't think it was possible to upset Marlee more than he already had. "It'll be all right," he said.

"If Frank hassles you in any way, let me know. Don't try to handle it yourself."

"Right." As if he'd run to Bernie for help. "I'll stay out of trouble," he said. "I won't do anything that might land me back inside."

"You do that." Bernie took his hands out of his pocket. "I guess I'd better head on home."

"Good night." Troy didn't bother seeing him to the door.

When Bernie was gone, Troy sank into the recliner and switched on the radio. The energetic voice of an announcer for the Houston Astros filled the room and he settled back to listen. He closed his eyes, and thought of another late spring night, when he'd lucked into tickets for a baseball game. He and Marlee had huddled in the nosebleed seats at the stadium, sharing a bag of peanuts and cheering home runs and double plays. They hadn't worried about the future, seeing the whole world colored rosy by their love.

Neither of them would ever be that naive again. But Troy prayed that some of those feelings might return. Their love had been the strongest and truest thing he'd ever known. He couldn't let himself believe even seven years apart was enough to kill it.

But what if Marlee never loved him again? Bernie's visit tonight had reminded Troy that he wasn't in control of anything. He could promise to live a good life, and to look after Greg and Marlee the way he should have all along—but if Marlee didn't believe him—or worse, if she no longer wanted the home and family they'd dreamed of before—then he was as helpless as if he'd never got out of jail.

"MARLEE, THERE'S A Troy Denton for you on line one."

Marlee started at the sound of Troy's name over

the intercom. She kept her personal life strictly separate from her job. At work, she was a calm, organized professional; she didn't talk about herself much, and no one knew much about her history. To have part of that past intrude on this world was unsettling. She snatched up the phone. "Hello?"

"Hi. Listen, I'm just a couple of blocks away and it's almost noon, so I thought I might stop by and take you to lunch." He spoke the words in a rush, then lapsed into silence.

She gripped the receiver tighter, fighting a nervous flutter in her stomach. Troy's request was innocent enough, but she didn't want him here. This was the area of her life where she felt most in control, and Troy made her doubt herself too much. "I don't think that's a good idea," she said.

"We need some time to talk without the chance that Greg will interrupt," he said.

"Talk about what?"

"Things. I'll pick you up in a few minutes." *Click.*

Marlee stared at the phone in her hand. He'd hung up on her.

"Is everything all right?" Mr. Morgenroth asked.

Is it? Marlee wondered. "Oh. Sure. That was a…uh, a friend. He's picking me up for lunch."

Mr. Morgenroth nodded and turned his attention back to his computer. "It's a nice day for it."

She grabbed her purse and hurried to the ladies' room to comb her hair and fix her makeup. As she searched in her bag for a comb, she was annoyed to discover her hands were trembling. *Snap out of it!* she silently scolded herself. *Whatever Troy has to say to you, you're still in charge of your life and of Greg's.* Maybe it *was* time they had a serious discussion about just what she expected from Troy in the future. So far he'd proved a good friend to Greg, and Marlee saw no sign that he intended to break the law again. But it was early days yet. She was right to be cautious.

She hurried from the bathroom, down the hall to the lobby. A woman's laughter, followed by the low rumble of a familiar male voice, drifted to her as she entered. Troy glanced up and smiled as she walked toward him. Marlee's heart stuttered. No matter how often she saw him, she couldn't get used to her physical reaction to him. Yes, he was good-looking, but the world was full of handsome men, and none of them made her feel this way.

He'd obviously succeeded in charming Trish. The clerk beamed at him, then at Marlee. "Troy was telling us about motorcycles," she said.

Marlee hadn't noticed Mr. Morgenroth. He stood on the other side of Troy, seemingly at ease with the man he had escorted from the hotel only the week before. "What do you know about the Gold Wing?" Mr. M. asked. "Is that a good choice for cross-country trips? Or would a Valkyrie be better?"

Troy rubbed his jaw, considering the question. "Well, now, either one would work as a touring bike, but for comfort, I prefer the Gold Wing."

"I've been doing some research, but I haven't had a chance to look at one close up," Mr. Morgenroth said.

Troy took a card from his wallet and handed it to the older man. "Come by the shop anytime. We specialize in custom bikes—sales and repairs. We'll fix you up, let you take a test ride."

"Mr. Morgenroth, I didn't know you were interested in motorcycles," Marlee said, unable to hide her surprise.

His face reddened. "Alice and I have been thinking about getting a bike for a while now, for taking out on weekends. They're very economical, you know."

She couldn't picture pudgy Mr. M. and his silver-haired wife straddling a chrome-and-leather monster.

"Your friend Troy here has given me a lot of helpful information," Mr. Morgenroth said, pocketing the business card.

So now Troy was her friend, when only last week his rough appearance had worried Mr. Morgenroth. What had changed? She studied the two men as they continued to talk. Was Mr. Morgenroth more accepting because Marlee was obviously comfortable enough to accompany Troy to lunch? Or did he give off a more easygoing vibe, less brittle and defensive than he'd been that first day?

"It was nice talking to you," Troy said. "Are you ready, Marlee?"

She nodded, and started toward the door. Troy moved ahead, and held it open for her. "I thought we'd walk over to the park and grab a hot dog from a cart, if that's okay," he said as they stepped into the bright sunshine. The heat was refreshing after the artificial chill of the air-conditioned hotel.

"That's fine."

They walked in silence to the corner. Marlee could feel his eyes on her as they waited for the light to change. "What did you want to talk about?" she asked, unable to bear the tension anymore.

"Let's wait until we get our food." The light turned green and they crossed. They stopped at a hot dog vendor parked beneath a spreading live oak. "One with everything," she ordered.

"Make that two." Troy stepped up behind her. If she leaned back just a little, she'd be able to rest her head against him, feel his arms encircle her. How odd that after so many years apart, his closeness still felt familiar. Almost natural.

She opened her purse, but before she could pull out her money, Troy had paid for the hot dogs and two soft drinks. Knowing it was useless to argue, she followed him to a shady spot beside a fountain.

At this hour, most of the picnic tables and benches were filled with workers from the nearby offices. Men shed their suit coats and women rolled up their sleeves in the warm spring sun. Mothers pushed strollers along the hike-and-bike trail beneath clouds of flowering pear trees, and students from the nearby University of Texas stretched out on the grass to study or nap.

But the peacefulness of the scene couldn't ease Marlee's worry over why Troy had asked for this meeting. "Tell me why it was so important we talk alone," she said when they were both seated at an empty picnic table in the shade of a massive oak.

"I think it's time to tell Greg the truth—that I'm his father."

"No!"

"Why not? He knows me now. He trusts me."

"He's not ready." *She* wasn't ready. Revealing that Troy was Greg's father would mean giving up being the only person Greg looked to for direction, guidance and support. Right now, Troy was just her son's friend. As a father, he'd have a much bigger role in both their lives. Could she really depend on him to be the kind of father her son deserved?

"He deserves to know the truth," Troy said. "It's going to be hard enough explaining why I wasn't around for the first six years of his life. It'll just get harder the longer we put it off."

"It's too soon. And he's so young—he won't understand."

"He won't understand that I'm his father? Or about why I went to prison? Or maybe he won't understand why we lied? He'll blame you, too, you know."

The thought of Greg turning on her was unbearable. There had to be a way to handle this situation that protected her son—and Marlee's relationship with him. "We'll tell him," she said. "But we need to take things slowly. We should talk about what role you'll have in his life."

"I'm his father. It's not a part in a play."

Marlee set aside her hot dog, uneaten. "Don't make this more difficult than it has to be, Troy," she said. "If we had a more conventional relationship—

if we were divorced, for instance—there'd be a court agreement to lay out visitation, parental rights and things like that. We need to discuss those issues."

."What's wrong with how we've been doing it? I'll see him whenever I can. And I'll pay you support to cover what he needs."

"I'd be more comfortable if we had a formal agreement," she said. "I want to know how we're going to share his time, have an idea of what our future looks like—and what you want from me."

"Then let's hire lawyers and make a formal agreement," he said. "I want what I've always wanted—for us to be a family. You, me and our son, living in a nice house in a good neighborhood, with money in a savings account for Greg's college, and vacations and barbecues on summer weekends."

The boldness of this statement, and the emotion behind the words, shook her. This was the dream they'd talked about when they'd first discovered she was pregnant. Well, *she'd* talked about it. In those days, Troy hadn't planned much. He talked about the future in vague terms. They would "see how things worked out" and "go with the flow."

Now he was repeating her dream back to her; obviously, he'd been listening to her after all. After Troy had been arrested, she'd vowed to give her son that life anyway, though Troy had no place in her new vision of the future. "You're talking about a dream I had in the past," she said. "That's not the future I want now."

"It's not the future you want—or not the future you think you can have?"

"I don't know what you're talking about."

"I mean—is it the dream that's wrong or is it me? What happens if you take me out of the picture? If you fell in love with some other man, wouldn't you want to get married, maybe even have more children?"

"I…I've been too busy to think about that." She'd been numb for so long. She'd poured all her energy and devotion into caring for Greg. The two of them were a family; she'd told herself she didn't need anyone else to be happy.

"When you wouldn't answer my letters, after a while I imagined you'd moved on. I didn't like the idea, but I knew a beautiful woman like you would have no trouble finding another man."

She said nothing. The last thing she'd wanted after what he'd put her through was a *man*. Men had brought her nothing but heartache.

"Maybe I've missed something," Troy continued "Are you dating someone now and I just haven't seen him? Did you recently break up with someone?"

"There isn't anyone and you know it. There hasn't been anyone." She met his gaze with a steady look of her own.

"Why is that—because you still had feelings for me, or because of how badly I hurt you?"

He was too close to the truth for her to risk acknowledging his question. Yes, he had hurt her, and yes, maybe deep down she did have some lingering feelings for him. She had happy memories of their time together as well as bad, and he had given her a son she cherished. But memories and affection for her child didn't mean she loved him, or that she would stake her future on him.

"I gave you an honest answer when I told you what I wanted from you," Troy said. "What do you want from me?"

"I don't want anything from you," she said. "I was doing just fine without you. I have a steady job and I'm saving money for a better house and for Greg's college. He's healthy and doing well in school. We have a good life."

"It sounds like a lonely one to me."

"I'm through with relying on someone else for my happiness."

He touched her hand, the slightest brush of his fingers across her knuckles. "Then I'm sorry for anything I did to make you feel that way."

The sweetness of the gesture and the words moved her, and she had to swallow past a sudden tightness in her throat. "We got off subject," she said. "We were talking about what's best for Greg."

"What's best is for us to tell him I'm his father."

"He's not ready," she repeated.

"Then how are you going to *get* him ready?"

"We'll— You'll become a bigger part of his life. See him more often. Really get to know him. Then, when you seem like one of the family, we'll tell him you *are* family."

"I'm all for seeing him more often. We can start this weekend."

"This weekend is our company picnic."

"I'll come with you. I assume you're allowed to bring guests."

"Yes, but…"

"But what?"

"I don't like people at work knowing about my personal life."

"Why not? They seem like nice people."

"I just… I like my privacy." The less people knew, the less they could use to judge her or to gossip about her, especially if things ever went wrong. Maybe *this* was the most lasting lesson her father had taught her—that it wasn't safe to reveal details about yourself to people, because the information might one day be used against you.

"They already know about me," Troy said. His tone lightened, his expression encouraging. "Maybe this is a way for you to get used to the idea that I'm going to be around for a long time."

She was tired of arguing with him; maybe she could give in on this one point. "All right. It's Saturday, in Zilker Park."

"I promise I'll make a good impression."

"You already impressed Trish and Mr. Morgenroth. What did you say to them before I got there?"

Troy took a bite of his hot dog and washed it down with a drink of soda before answering. "I wasn't in the lobby two seconds before your boss came out of his office and started peppering me with questions."

"What kind of questions?"

"Oh, the usual—where did I work? How long had I known you? He didn't exactly ask me if my intentions were honorable, but I could tell he wanted to. He obviously thinks a lot of you."

She smiled. "Mr. Morgenroth watches out for all of us."

"I got the impression you were special to him, though."

"I think he felt sorry for me when I first applied for a job after Greg was born. A lot of other places wouldn't even consider me because I was so young, and a single mother. Mr. Morgenroth gave me a chance to prove myself. I always felt he really wanted me to succeed."

"I'm glad you had someone to look out for you."

"It felt good to be able to take care of myself." For all the pain that Troy's arrest caused, it had also taught her that she was strong enough to survive on her own.

Troy finished his hot dog and tossed the wrapper in the trash. "Are you going to eat?" he asked.

She shook her head and threw her hot dog in the trash after his wrapper. "I'm not hungry."

"Then let's walk."

They set off on a path across the park. Two women in purple sports bras and wind shorts jogged toward them. A trio of businessmen eating lunch nearby paused their conversation to ogle the pair. Marlee glanced at Troy, to see if he was doing the same. But his eyes were fixed on her. She still couldn't believe he'd admitted he wanted them to be a couple—a family? He wasn't saying he *loved* her, was he? Not after all this time. She hadn't answered his letters so she could try to forget about him—and she'd assumed he'd eventually done the same.

"Hey, Denton! Man, how's it goin'?"

Beside her, Troy stiffened. Marlee followed his gaze to the bleary-eyed panhandler shuffling toward them. The young man wore ragged jeans and a dirty flannel shirt, and carried a knapsack and blanket roll on his back. His hair was long and matted and he needed a shave. "Good to see a friendly face, man." The derelict clapped Troy on the shoulder. Troy froze, as though turned to stone.

The man looked around Troy to Marlee. "Hello, ma'am." He nodded and held out a filthy hand. "Name's Richard Scott, though most folks call me Scotty."

Marlee stared at the handmade tattoo that snaked across the back of the man's hand. The crude combination of symbols and letters made her shiver. Her father had had similar markings. As a little girl, she'd been fascinated by "Daddy's pictures." Later, she'd learned about jailhouse tattoos, and had been ashamed that her father wore these symbols that marked him as a criminal.

Scotty must have sensed her hesitation. He jerked his hand away and wiped it on his jeans. "Don't know what I's thinkin'—gonna get you all dirty." He turned to Troy, who was staring at him, clench-jawed. "Say, you lookin' good, man. Outside world ain't been so kind to old Scotty."

"Listen, we'd better go." Troy jerked his wallet from his pocket and pulled out a twenty. "Good luck, man." He pressed the bill into Scotty's hand, then grabbed Marlee's arm and hurried her along the path.

"Friend of yours?" she asked. She looked back over her shoulder. Scotty hadn't moved, staring at the twenty in his hand.

"Just…nobody. Just nobody." He spat out the words.

"You knew him in prison," she said.

"We'd better head for the hotel. Your boss won't be so impressed with me if I bring you back late."

"Not until you tell me the truth. Did you know that guy in prison?"

"Yes, I knew him in prison. It's not something I like being reminded of, okay?"

He started walking again, and she hurried to keep up. The contrast between the tattooed panhandler and the man beside her was startling. They had come from the same place, released with the standard provisions of a hundred dollars and a change of clothes—or at least, that had been the program years ago when her father was part of her life. Scotty had apparently done what many cons did—blown through the money and ended up with nothing to show for it. Likely as not, he'd be locked up again in a few weeks or months, and the cycle would continue.

Troy, on the other hand, had a job, transportation and a place to live. He was rebuilding his life, making amends to the people he'd hurt, proving that he was the exception to the rule.

She'd been so blinded by her prejudice against her father and his associates that she'd failed to see that until now. "Maybe it's good to be reminded sometimes," she said.

He shot her a fierce look. "Why? So I'll know my place?"

"No. So you'll know how far you've come." She put a hand on his arm. "You're not like Scotty. And…and you're not like my dad, either. I can see that now."

Some of the anger left his eyes, and he covered her hand with his own. They walked in silence back to the hotel, but she knew they'd reached a kind of truce this afternoon. She was closer to understanding the man Troy had become, and maybe he was more accepting of the choices she'd made. They hadn't resolved all their differences, but they'd made a start. If he wanted more from her than friendship, he'd be disappointed. She was confident now that they would find a middle ground where they could be the parents Greg needed. But she'd lost herself too completely to him before, and paid too high a price when things went wrong. She wouldn't take that kind of risk again.

CHAPTER SEVEN

TROY LEFT MARLEE outside the hotel's main entrance, but instead of getting on his motorcycle and returning to his own job, he crossed the street and returned to the park. The encounter with Scotty had shaken him. All he wanted was to forget the previous seven years had ever happened—to replace the grim memories of prison with a new, happier life. But reminders—like Bernie, and now Scotty—kept intruding.

He would have to learn to live with Bernie's presence, but he could definitely do something about Scotty.

He passed the hot dog vender and thought of the lunch Marlee hadn't touched. She'd probably grab something at her office once she was calmer. He hadn't accomplished what he'd hoped for with their lunch, but she was warming up to him. He'd settle for that for now.

One reason he liked his job at the garage was because it involved taking things that were broken and making them work. Customers came in with a problem and he was able to solve it. The results were evident and tangible.

He'd thought talking to Marlee today would be

like that. He had a problem—keeping his identity from Greg—and he would solve it by confronting Marlee.

But women obviously weren't motorcycles. And he didn't yet have the right tools to bring her around to his point of view.

And Marlee wasn't just a woman, but also a mother. She knew their son better than Troy did, and if she believed revealing the truth now would harm Greg, Troy had to accept that. The last thing he wanted was to hurt Greg, or to damage the bond that was growing between them.

But even though Marlee was a wonderful mother, Greg needed a father, too. As he got older, there would be more and more situations where he'd need a man's perspective. A mom could help, but only a dad could really know what went through a boy's head when he walked into the locker room the first day of junior high. A dad would understand the way boys judged each other's physical prowess and reputation.

Troy wanted to be there for his son whenever Greg needed him.

And what about Troy's relationship with Marlee? He'd clearly caught her off guard by declaring that he wanted the three of them to be a family, but she seemed angry. He counted that as a minor victory.

He crested a small hill and spotted Scotty shuffling along a path by the lake. He and Troy had been cellmates for a time, then on the same block for several years. Troy never thought of his fellow inmates as friends, but Scotty was as close to one as he ever came. He jogged down the hill. "Scotty, wait up."

Scotty turned. "Hey, Denton!" He pulled the twenty from his pocket. "Come for your change?"

"No, man, it's all yours."

"Thought maybe you was tryin' to impress your girl."

Troy shrugged. He doubted Marlee had been impressed, but her attitude toward him had definitely softened after their encounter with Scotty. Her admission that he wasn't like her father was a huge step forward. He owed Scotty thanks for his contribution to that transformation.

"How'd you end up like this, Scotty?"

"You know how it is, man. It's hard on the outside—no money, no job. I'm not like you. I don't have any kind of mechanical skills, or anything else."

"If you'd thought about that while you were inside, you could've learned something. You could've taken classes, or enrolled in job training. You could've had a plan."

Scotty laughed. "You sound like my parole officer. So how's *your* plan working out for you?"

"Okay, I guess."

"What was it? Maybe I can learn by example."

"My plan was to get a job, a bike and a place to live. And then I was going to put my family back together. That's the part I'm still working on."

"You got family? Your mom and dad around here somewhere?"

Troy shook his head. "My dad's dead and my mom and I don't talk that much. Everybody else is scattered."

"Sounds like my folks. They're all up north somewhere. None of them have anything to do with me."

"You know what the hardest thing was about being locked up?"

"Aside from the rotten food, sadistic guards and crazy inmates?"

"The hardest thing was being so alone—away from anyone who cared about me, or anyone I cared about." When he met Marlee, he'd been drifting emotionally for a year, since his father's death. He'd felt empty inside, unsure of what he should do with his life. Her love had anchored him and given him a purpose. When she'd gotten pregnant, that purpose had strengthened. He wanted to be there for her and for their baby the way his father had always been there for him.

His love for her and Greg still anchored him now. Life wasn't perfect, but he would work with what he had.

Right now, Scotty needed help. He nodded to the crumpled bill in Scotty's hand. "What do you plan to do with that money?"

Scotty considered the bill. "Score some dope maybe. Or buy a couple cases of beer and stay drunk for a week."

"Is that what you really want to do?"

He shrugged. "You got a better idea?"

Troy looked him up and down. "How about a bath and a shave? Some clean clothes? Maybe a job?"

Scotty laughed, a sharp, barking sound. "Where am I gonna get all that for a double sawbuck? Besides, who's gonna hire a con like me?"

"*Ex*-con." Troy shoved one hand into his pocket. "I can help with the bath and clothes. And my boss is looking for somebody to clean up around the shop. He'll give you a chance, if you're willing to take it."

Scotty stared at the twenty. People flowed around them on the trail, like water around a rock in a creek bed. "Why do you even want to take a chance on me?" he asked.

"It's not much of a chance. My boss sometimes hires ex-cons and he needs help right now. I can introduce you, but whether or not you get the job is up to you."

"And if I do you've done your good deed for the day?"

"Yeah, I'm a regular Boy Scout. Do you want to do this or not?"

Scotty shoved the twenty into his pocket. "Why not? I got nothing better going on."

As declarations went, it wasn't enthusiastic, but Troy hadn't expected enthusiasm. A lot of the guys he'd met in prison were like that—so used to being disappointed by life they'd stopped caring. Without the memory of Marlee's love—and the knowledge of how good life could be—he might have ended up the same way.

SATURDAY MORNING, Marlee hurried to put the finishing touches on the cake she was bringing to the company picnic, while Greg raced from room to room. "I'm ready to go, Mom!" he shouted, then almost collided with Troy as he entered the kitchen from the back door.

"I put the cooler in the car," Troy said. "Can I do anything else?"

"You could grab that stack of towels, and the bag with the bathing suits. Oh, and I need to get sunscreen. And a hat. Greg has to have a hat."

"I'll get my hat, Mom," Greg called as he raced past once more.

"This icing isn't going on as smooth as it's supposed to," Marlee said. "Troy, does the cake look all right? I knew I should have made it last night, but I wanted it to be as fresh as possible."

"The cake looks great. Delicious." He stood behind her and rested his hands on her shoulders. "Relax," he said. "It's a picnic. A fun day in the park. Things don't have to be perfect."

"It's a day with all my coworkers," she said. "I don't want to embarrass myself."

He leaned around her and swiped his index finger through the frosting left in the mixing bowl. "Mmm," he said, sucking the chocolate off his finger. "Delicious."

It was a playful gesture—and a sexy one, too. Just when Marlee had convinced herself she could think of Troy only as a friend, he would do something like this and remind her that the connection between them hadn't disappeared completely. No matter how hard she tried to ignore it, Troy had once meant a great deal to her and she couldn't pretend otherwise.

"Is there bottled water in the cooler?" she asked, picking up the spatula again and adding more frosting to the cake. "And plenty of ice?"

"Yes to both. And soda and juice, too. There's a roll of paper towels in the backseat, and wet wipes, insect repellent and a first-aid kit in the glove box. You've got enough supplies for a week-long camping trip, so we should survive a day in the park."

"You never know what could happen. I like to be prepared." Marlee admitted she was probably over-doing it, but the only way she knew to get past the anxiety she felt in new situations was to be as prepared as possible.

"Are you nervous because I'm going with you today?" Troy asked.

"I'm always nervous about this kind of thing," she said.

"A picnic?"

"I told you, I don't like mixing my personal and professional lives." She stepped back to examine the cake. It looked a little better. It would have to do.

"Why is that? You spend so much time at work, it seems like it would be hard to keep them from overlapping."

"It's not, really. I don't talk about my life much at the office. If people don't know a lot about me, they can't ask nosy questions."

"What kind of questions?"

"We really don't have time to talk about this." She settled the cover carefully over the cake in its carrier.

"We have a few minutes. Greg's still in his room, looking for his hat. And I'd like to know. What kind of questions do people ask?"

"They want to know where I'm from. Where was I born? Where did I grow up? Where did I go to school? Do I have family in Austin?"

"And you don't want to talk about that."

"No! I never even told people in school about my father. Though they found out anyway."

The lines around his eyes deepened as he looked at her with compassion. "Was that hard for you?"

She nodded. "I lost friends over it. People whose parents didn't want their children associating with me or my family. I don't want that happening to Greg, so I keep my past a secret."

"Are you worried what people will say about me today?"

"Yes." She'd hardly slept last night, imagining worst-case scenarios—everything from Scotty crashing the picnic to reminisce about old times behind bars, to her father appearing and regaling everyone with tales of his exploits. Of course, there was no chance of either of those things happening, but in the dark hours after midnight her imagination ran away with her. "People have asked me about you before," she said. "Well, not you specifically, but they ask if I was married before. They want to know what happened. Am I in touch with Greg's father? Does he pay child support? Has he remarried? Nothing is off limits for some people."

"What do you tell them?" Troy asked.

"It depends on who it is. Sometimes I say I don't want to talk about it. Sometimes I tell the truth—that I was never married and we haven't had contact since before Greg was born." That statement had earned her some shocked reactions and a few disapproving looks. If people probed further—if they wanted to know what happened, where the father was now, how she felt about him—she refused to elaborate. Eventually, people got tired of asking.

"You don't have to worry about me today," Troy said. "I won't say anything about the past or about us. I'm a friend of yours and I'm attending the picnic as your guest."

"They'll think we're dating." Why else would a single woman invite a man to a company function?

"Would that be so horrible?"

Maybe not horrible—after all, Troy was good-looking and kind. A lot of women would be thrilled to date a man like him. But as wonderful as Troy could be, he was still an ex-con. Every time he applied for a loan or a new job, every time he renewed his driver's license or leased an apartment, that record would be there, a big, black mark. She'd lived that kind of life once—she didn't want any part of it again.

"I found my hat!" Greg raced back into the kitchen, holding up a black Austin Ice Bats ball cap.

Marlee's heart contracted as she watched her son

settle the hat on his head, looking first to her, then to Troy for approval. At one time, she couldn't imagine loving anyone more than she'd loved Troy. But when Greg was born, she'd been overwhelmed by a different kind of love. She would have done anything to ensure her boy grew up safe and happy.

"You look great, sport," Troy said.

Marlee checked the clock and let out a groan. "We're going to be late," she said. "We need to finish loading the car."

"I'll get the towels!" Greg grabbed the stack and raced for the door.

Marlee picked up the cake and started after him, but Troy stopped her. "Can I say something?" he asked.

"What?" He looked so serious, which made him seem stronger somehow.

"I met some of your coworkers the other day," he said "They seem to be nice people. They really like you. I don't think they're judging you as harshly as you think."

"So I'm silly to worry? Too cautious?"

"No. I think you have solid reasons to feel the way you do. But the past doesn't necessarily predict the future."

An odd thing to say, coming from a man who had confessed to wanting to recapture the dreams they'd had in the past. At the time, she'd been amazed that he would think they could ever pick up where they'd left off.

Now, she wondered. Maybe what Troy really

wanted was something better than what they could have had before. They'd both matured. They'd made mistakes, but they'd learned from them.

Could she and Troy negotiate their new relationship? She still wasn't sure what that relationship was—how she *wanted* it to be defined. But they weren't enemies and he was, in fact, proving to be a good friend. He cared about what she thought and how she felt, even if he did have an annoying habit of assuming he knew best.

She wanted to trust him, and she was willing to try.

AT ZILKER PARK, Troy helped Marlee carry the supplies to the picnic area reserved for hotel employees. Several of her coworkers cast curious glances in his direction, but Marlee avoided looking at any of them. "Greg, put those napkins over there by the plates," she directed. "Troy, the cooler should go at the end of the table. And do you think the cake will be okay here?"

"Mom, what's wrong with you?" Greg asked. "Why are you acting all weird?"

"I'm not acting weird," she said. "I just want everything to be right."

It upset Troy to see Marlee in such a state because she was worried about what her coworkers might think of her. Had his leaving done this to her? Or was he giving himself too much credit? Maybe raising a child alone had made Marlee more guarded.

A woman and a girl a little older than Greg approached. "Hello, Marlee," the woman said. "Did you make that cake? It looks wonderful."

"Thanks. Um, Peggy Jarvis, this is my friend Troy Denton."

"Nice to meet you." Troy shook hands with Peggy and soon he was being introduced to half a dozen other people. They all greeted him warmly, and he noticed Marlee's shoulders relax.

Mr. Morgenroth approached. Dressed in a blue polo shirt and khaki shorts with a floppy canvas hat shading his head, he looked more like a golf-playing grandfather than a business executive. "Troy! Good to see you." He looked over to the parking lot. "Did you ride your bike? It's a great day for it."

"No, I came with Marlee and Greg." Marlee had moved farther down the long picnic table beneath the pavilion, where she and a group of women, including Peggy and Trish, were arranging bowls of food and stacks of plates. Greg and the little girl had joined a group of kids on the playscape nearby.

"Marlee said you were an old friend," Mr. Morgenroth said.

That was as good a way as any to describe their relationship. "Yeah. We knew each other years ago."

"Marlee never talks much about herself," Mr. Morgenroth mused.

Troy remembered her earlier assertion that sharing too much about one's past only led to more questions. "She's a very private person," he said.

"And I respect that. Marlee has always been special to me."

"She said you hired her when no one else would. She's very grateful for that."

"Over the years I've learned that attitude and intelligence can count for more than work experience and education," Mr. Morgenroth explained. "When Marlee came to that first interview she was nervous but determined. She said she was trying to build a new life for herself and I wanted to help her."

"She has that effect on people." Yet Marlee could never see it. She mistook their goodwill for pity or judgment. When he'd first met her, she'd used a teenage brazenness as a defense against others getting too close. The adult Marlee was doing the same thing, using her privacy and fierce independence to keep out the rest of the world—even him.

"We have a mentoring program in the company, where a junior employee shadows a senior one to learn the ins and outs of the job," Mr. Morgenroth said. "The idea is not only to teach, but to develop close relationships so that the junior employee has an advocate higher-up, someone who is familiar with her strengths and weaknesses, and can be a sounding board. I've recommended Marlee for the program. I think it could really help her career, but for some reason she's reluctant to participate."

Marlee had talked so much about building a better life for herself and Greg, Troy was surprised she hadn't taken advantage of this opportunity to advance. Was it the words *close relationship* that frightened her away?

"Troy! Troy, watch me!"

A shout from the playscape drew their attention. Troy turned in time to see Greg shoot down the tallest slide. He grinned and waved. "Way to go!" he called as the boy hit the dirt at the end of the slide and raced back to the ladder for another try. Troy didn't think he'd ever tire of watching his son do even simple things like this.

Trish waved from the picnic tables. "Come on, everyone!" she called. "It's time to eat!"

"Troy! Come sit with me!" Greg ran to take Troy's hand then tugged him toward the tables. They fell in line behind Mr. Morgenroth and filled their plates with barbecue, potato salad, coleslaw and beans.

Marlee joined them in the line. "Honey, don't take more than you can eat," she cautioned as Greg heaped food onto his plate.

"Save some room for your mom's cake," Troy said, scraping half of Greg's potato salad onto his own plate.

The three of them settled at the table across from Trish and Mr. Morgenroth. As he ate, Troy studied Marlee's coworkers. Though she claimed not to be close to them, these were as near to a family as she had. He thought of his own family, aunts and uncles and cousins scattered around the country and largely estranged. For so long, he'd thought he only needed Marlee and Greg to be complete. Now he saw that a larger circle—of friends or family—could provide the support and help everyone needed. The more people around, the more likely everyone was to succeed. As much as he hated to admit that Bernie was right, this kind of social-support system probably was key to making it on the outside.

Troy glanced at Marlee, who sat on the other side of Greg, helping the boy cut a slice of brisket. Her head was bent close to his, almost touching, as she guided his hands in hers. She could have accomplished the task more quickly by taking over and doing it herself, but Greg had probably insisted on cutting his own meat, so this was a compromise.

Maybe that was the trick to reaching Marlee, Troy thought. Don't infringe on the independence she valued so highly, but make sure she knew he was there if she needed him. He didn't want to take over her life or make decisions for her; he only wanted to be beside her, to show her that two people together could be stronger than one person alone.

The Reader Service — Here's how it works:

NO POSTAGE
NECESSARY
IF MAILED
IN THE
UNITED STATES

BUSINESS REPLY MAIL

FIRST-CLASS MAIL   PERMIT NO. 717   BUFFALO, NY

POSTAGE WILL BE PAID BY ADDRESSEE

THE READER SERVICE
PO BOX 1867
BUFFALO NY 14240-9952

GET FREE BOOKS & FREE GIFTS WHEN YOU PLAY THE...

Lucky

777

SLOT MACHINE GAME

Just scratch off the gold box with a coin.
Then check below to see the gifts you get!

YES! I have scratched off the gold box. Please send me the 2 free Harlequin® Superromance® books and 2 free gifts (gifts are worth about $10) for which I qualify. I understand I am under no obligation to purchase any books, as explained on the back of this card.

We want to make sure we offer you the best service suited to your needs. Please answer the following question:

About how many NEW paperback fiction books have you purchased in the past 3 months?

❏ 0-2	❏ 3-6	❏ 7 or more
E4NQ	E37P	E37Z

❏ I prefer the regular-print edition   ❏ I prefer the larger-print edition
135/336 HDL   139/339 HDL

FIRST NAME   LAST NAME

ADDRESS

APT.   CITY

STATE /PROV.   ZIP/POSTAL CODE

Visit us online at
www.ReaderService.com

7	7	7	**Worth TWO FREE BOOKS plus 2 BONUS Mystery Gifts!**
🍒	🍒	🍒	**Worth TWO FREE BOOKS!**
🔔	🔔	🍒	**TRY AGAIN!**

CHAPTER EIGHT

AFTER LUNCH, Mr. Morgenroth, tireless in his role of host, gathered the children together for a game of volleyball. Marlee and Troy sat in lawn chairs in the shade and watched the game. "Hey, that was great!" Troy applauded as Greg launched the ball over the net with a little help from Mr. M.

He's so focused on Greg, so proud of him, Marlee thought. Would people guess he was more than a friend? Every day it was harder to convince herself she was doing the right thing by delaying telling Greg the truth—but at the same time, every day that passed made it more difficult to admit she had deliberately lied to him.

Troy turned and caught her staring. "You look so serious," he said. "Is something wrong?"

She shook her head. "You surprise me."

"How is that?"

"The way you get along so well with Greg. I've never known any men who were that into kids."

"Greg isn't just any kid."

"When you first came back, I was sure you'd get bored after a few weeks, or that you'd make a couple token gestures and leave again."

"You thought that or you hoped that?"

Was she so transparent? Or was it only that Troy knew her so well? "I don't think any mother relishes sharing her responsibilities with someone else—especially someone who's just been released from prison."

"I hope I've proved you don't have anything to worry about."

"I always worry. It's part of being a mother. And part of who I am."

Troy sat back in his chair. They were sitting a little apart from the others, but he lowered his voice further, so as not to be overheard. "Mr. Morgenroth told me about a mentoring program at your work. He thinks you'd be perfect for it."

Her mouth tightened. "It's none of your concern."

"Why won't you join the program?" he pushed.

Why did he insist on being so...so *involved* in her life?

"It sounds like a great opportunity," he said.

"It requires long hours and some travel. I can't be away from Greg that much."

"You could make arrangements for him. I could look after him."

She waited for the familiar, panicky feeling she got whenever she thought of leaving her son with someone else, but it didn't come. Troy would no doubt take good care of Greg, and Greg would love spending time with him. She would miss him, but she certainly wouldn't be afraid for his safety or health.

"I just don't think I'd enjoy the program," she said. The brochure Mr. Morgenroth gave her had included testimonials from previous participants, who talked about the "close, personal relationships" they'd built with their mentors. Photographs showed two women laughing as they bent over papers at a conference table, and a younger and older man dressed for golf. The idea of opening her life to someone else made Marlee's heart race.

"It's the privacy thing, isn't it?" Troy asked.

She shrugged. "I'm not the kind of person who wants to be chummy with my superiors."

"I can understand that. But you know you don't have anything to be ashamed of, don't you?"

My father was a career criminal. I had a baby out of wedlock while the baby's father was in jail. Maybe they weren't big things to most people, but to Marlee they were like the secret she was keeping from Greg—the longer she remained silent, the more difficult it was to confess.

It wasn't only her past she didn't care to reveal, however. Getting close to someone guaranteed heartache. Sooner or later, people disappointed you, went away or died—the way her father, Troy and her mother had done. She was tired of being abandoned that way.

"I can't believe Mr. Morgenroth told you about the mentoring program," she said.

"He cares about you. I think he wanted me to know it—like a dad warning a boyfriend not to step out of line."

Marlee felt her cheeks heat. "Does he think you're my boyfriend?"

"He didn't say, but you can't keep people from speculating."

No, though she'd certainly tried.

TROY HOPED Marlee's coworkers did think they were a couple. Maybe their acceptance would help Marlee decide to let him closer. She spoke of protecting Greg from the censure of those who might disapprove of her father's or Troy's past, but she was clearly protecting herself as well. How could he convince her he wouldn't let anyone hurt her or their son?

"Come on, let's go swimming." As the volleyball game wound down, Trish rose from her chair and waved to the players. "Anyone want to take a dip in Barton Springs?"

"I do!" Greg bounded toward them and launched himself into Marlee's lap. "Can we go swimming, Mom? Please?"

"Yes, we can go swimming." She hugged him tight, burying her nose in his neck and inhaling deeply.

"Mo-om!" Giggling, he squirmed out of her lap and ran to Troy. "Let's go swimming. Now!"

They collected their towels and swimsuits from the car and started up the path to the pool. "Greg, you come with me," Marlee said, heading toward the women's changing room.

"But, Mom, I don't want to change in the ladies' room!" Greg scowled at Marlee and knotted his swim trunks in his hands.

"He can come with me." Troy winked at the boy. "After all, we men have to stick together."

Marlee frowned, but then nodded. "All right. Greg, you stay with Troy. This is a big place and I don't want you wandering off."

"I'm not a baby," Greg protested.

Troy caught his hand. "She knows you're not a baby," he said. "She's just being a mom. You wouldn't want her to get thrown out of the moms' union for not doing her job, would you?"

Greg laughed and looked up at Marlee, who was trying hard to maintain her frown, but not quite succeeding. "Moms' union!" She shook her head, laughter escaping. "Where do you come up with this stuff?"

He waggled his eyebrows and grinned. "You wouldn't want me to give away all my secrets, now, would you?"

Their gazes met and held. Troy had a sudden vision of what it would be like if they were a real family—the laughter, the shared jokes. He and Greg could go swimming together all the time. Then later, when the swimming was over and Greg had gone to bed, he and Marlee...

"Come on, Troy, hurry!"

The boy swinging on his arm pulled him out of his fog of longing, back to the park with its summer Saturday crowd. Marlee turned away, toward the women's dressing room. "Meet you at the pool," she said, and slipped into the dank concrete bunker.

Troy helped Greg strip out of his shorts and into a pair of red-and-black trunks that bagged to his knees. Then, while Greg hopped impatiently from bench to floor and back, Troy dressed in his own purple trunks. He'd bought them only this morning, and had to pause to tear off the price tag.

They stowed their clothes in a locker and Troy pinned the key to his trunks. "Now are we ready?" Greg asked.

Troy grinned at him. "We're ready."

They emerged into the sunlight at the side of Barton Springs Swimming Pool. The spring-fed, rock-bottomed swimming hole attracted swimmers of all ages year-round, from octogenarians in swim caps and Speedos to UT students in bandannas and tie-dye. The constant sixty-five-degree water provided a cooling dip for scorching summer days and an invigorating workout on winter mornings. For many people, Barton Springs was as much a symbol of Austin as armadillos and bats. For Troy, coming to this pool was like coming home.

He followed Greg to the shallow end, where Marlee and Trish waited. The women sat on the edge of the pool, dangling their feet in the water. Troy caught his breath at the sight of Marlee in her bright pink tank suit. His memory hadn't done justice to her body, which teased his senses now with ripe curves and swelling breasts sheathed in Lycra.

His reaction was immediate and obvious in the purple trunks. He slipped into the water, grateful for the shock of cold, which tempered his desire. He waded over to Marlee and Trish. "The water's just as cold as it ever was," he said.

Marlee appeared to be watching Greg splash in the shallows. But her cheeks had a flush that had nothing to do with the sun, as if she was aware of him and his eyes on her. He willed her to look at him, and she did, eyes heavy-lidded and dark.

"I'm going for a swim," she said. "Trish, will you keep an eye on Greg?"

"Sure," Trish said.

Marlee dived into the water and glided past Troy. She'd always been a strong swimmer. Troy plunged his head underwater and surfaced, then settled into long, easy strokes across the pool. Together, they headed for the peninsula of rock that jutted out near the diving board. He hauled himself out of the water and held out a hand for Marlee.

He pulled her up beside him, almost into his lap. She settled a few inches away and wrung the water from her hair. Droplets cascaded down her shoulders, sliding between her breasts.

They had spent the day in each other's company, but being with her now felt more intimate than all the time before. Maybe it was because they were barely dressed, or the pool itself and the memories associated with it worked a spell on them.

"Do you remember when we used to come here?" Troy asked. Their last summer together, they had spent practically every Sunday afternoon here. They'd tease each other in the water, with furtive touches and whispered promises, until, aching with desire, they'd rush home to make love, their cool clammy skin heating and drying in the warmth of their passion.

"I'd never forget. It was always one of my favorite places." She hugged her knees to her chest. "Those were some of my favorite times."

"Remembering times like that got me through my worst days in prison," he said.

"Was it very bad for you?" She tilted her head, resting her cheek on one knee to look at him. "Whenever my father talked about doing time, it was like it was some privileged club for tough guys."

"He wouldn't have told you the bad stuff," Troy said. "He wanted you to respect him."

"So it *was* bad," she said.

"It wasn't good. Prison isn't just about taking away your freedom. When you're inside, you also lose your privacy and your dignity. Some guys lose their minds."

"But you didn't."

"No. I figured out quickly that it helped to focus on something else—something outside those walls. For some guys it was religion. Others wanted revenge. For me it was you and our baby."

Her eyes shone and she blinked rapidly. "Even after I didn't answer your letters?"

"I had a responsibility to you, no matter what."

"So that's what kept you going—a sense of responsibility?"

"No. What kept me going was love."

"Love?" She repeated the word as if she'd never heard it before. "After seven years with no contact? That's crazy."

"Maybe it is a little bit, but that's how I feel." He

sensed her pulling away, and he struggled to keep her with him. "I'm not trying to pressure you. I'm just being honest. I love you and I love Greg. I want to be with you and to give you the kind of life I promised before. If you don't feel the same about me, I'll be Greg's father and help you whenever you need me. But if you think there's a chance for us, then I'm willing to wait." There had been moments when they'd been alone together—when they'd caught each other's eyes, when he'd kissed her—that he'd been sure she still felt something for him. She said there had been no other man in her life. Was that really because she didn't want a relationship, or because her heart belonged to him?

She opened her mouth, closed it again, then shook her head. "You'll always be special to me," she said. "You were my first love, and you're Greg's father. But too much has happened since then for us to go back."

"I'm not suggesting going back," he said. "I want us to move forward. To start over together."

"I…" She put a hand over his and squeezed it briefly, then released it. "We're friends. Let's leave it at that for now." Then she slipped into the water and swam back across the pool.

He let her go, watching until she climbed out on the other side next to Greg and Trish. He supposed he should be grateful. She didn't hate him and was willing to let him be a part of her life, which was a big improvement over where they'd been five weeks ago. But it wasn't enough. He wanted more than friendship from Marlee. More than being her son's father and meeting up to trade custody. He'd returned to her believing he could rekindle the love she'd once had for him.

Instead, maybe he needed to start from scratch— to build a new love between them. One that was stronger than Marlee's doubts and fears or the past that haunted them still.

MARLEE SPLASHED in the water with Greg, but every part of her was aware of Troy, across the pool. He sat on the rocks like a brooding Greek god risen from the waters. He'd said he loved her as if it was the most logical thing in the world. The idea that his love for her had survived for seven years with no encouragement both touched and frightened her. What could be more romantic? But how in the world could she live up to that kind of emotion?

The day she'd learned Troy had been convicted, she'd forced herself to put aside her love for him, as if it was a family heirloom that she'd packed in a box and set out at the curb for the garbage collectors. She told herself she was done with Troy and with love.

Now both were back in her life and she didn't know what to do. He was Greg's father, so she couldn't send him away and, truthfully, she no longer wanted to.

She just wanted her life the way it was before he showed up—uncomplicated. Predictable. Controlled.

Sure, things were going well, but in her experience, that only meant something bad was waiting around the corner. As a child, every time she'd begin to believe her dad would stay home and they'd be a real family, he'd get arrested and disappear from their lives again. Then she met Troy and thought she might finally have the family she'd dreamed of, but that hadn't lasted either. If she let Troy back into her life now, how long before things soured again?

Seated in the water beside her, Greg yawned loudly. "You've had a big day, haven't you?" Marlee said. "Are you ready to go?"

"No, I want to stay," he said, but it was a token protest.

Marlee stood and helped him to his feet. "Come on. Let's get changed and go gather up our picnic stuff."

As they walked around the side of the pool, she spotted Troy ahead of them, just disappearing into the men's changing rooms. "Go on inside with Troy," she told Greg. "I'll meet you out here when you're done."

Ten minutes later she was back outside, warmer and dryer, her wet hair in a French braid trailing down her back. Trish stood by the low concrete wall that separated the pool from the dressing rooms. "Where's the G-man?" she asked.

"Getting changed with Troy." Marlee adjusted her grip on her tote bag.

"I thought he was with you."

She turned and found Troy leaning against the wall behind her. "I saw him go into the men's room, right behind you," she said.

"I never saw him."

Marlee felt her panic rising and fought for control. "He has to be here somewhere." She frantically scanned the area near the pool. But there was no sign of Greg in the crush of people in and around the water.

Troy turned to Trish. "Why don't you walk over to the picnic tables and see if you spot him on the way."

Trish nodded. "I'll get some of the others to search with us."

Trish sprinted toward the picnic grounds. Troy put his hand on Marlee's shoulder. His warm strength seemed to flow into her, steadying her somehow. She looked into his eyes again. He tried to reassure her. "We'll find him, Marl. We will."

She swallowed and nodded, tears clogging her throat.

"I'll check the pool," he said. "Maybe he decided to go back in."

"I'll come with you."

He shook his head. "No, you wait here, in case he's trying to find you."

"All right." She watched him walk away. When he disappeared around the corner, she hugged her arms across her chest and fought back tears. Where was her baby? The thought of losing Greg made her ice cold all over.

She stared at the door to the men's room, scarcely daring to blink. She'd seen Greg go inside, she was sure. So where was he now?

Trish ran up, Mr. Morgenroth in tow. "Any sign of him?" Mr. M.'s face was gray with worry.

Marlee shook her head, unable to speak. She glanced toward the pool.

"There he is!"

Mr. Morgenroth pointed to the pool entrance, but Marlee had already spotted Greg and Troy. Her son rode on Troy's shoulders, clutching a handful of Troy's hair in one hand, the other hand curled into a tight fist.

Marlee pushed her way toward them. "Where have you been?" She put one hand on Greg's knee, as if to prove he was safe.

"I had to get my rock collection." He opened his hand to reveal an array of colored stones.

"He was standing in the shallows picking up rocks when I found him," Troy said. "He must have slipped out of the change room when neither of us was looking."

Marlee was shaky with relief. Only the presence of her colleagues around them kept her from throwing her arms around Troy and thanking him for finding her baby.

She saw how tightly he held Greg, and read emotion in his gaze that matched her own. He handed the boy to her, but his eyes lingered on the child.

She realized how glad she was that Troy had been with her just now. She'd never known how good it could be to have another person share the pain and burdens of parenthood as well as the joy. For a brief moment she could see a different picture of the future. Maybe she'd made a mistake in protecting herself so much. Maybe she did have room in her life for someone else—as long as that someone was Troy.

"SO THIS IS WHERE you work."

At the sound of the familiar feminine voice, Troy peered out from behind the engine housing of a '44 Triumph. His gaze traveled up black slacks covering firm thighs and a trim waist to a pale yellow blouse, and finally came to rest on Marlee's face.

He stood and reached for a rag to wipe the grease from his hands. "What are you doing here, Marlee?"

She ran her hand along the seat of a 1948 Harley Panhead parked by the door. "Maybe I wanted to buy a motorcycle."

"That one's not for sale." He pushed himself away from the bench and walked over to a '96 Honda Royal Star. It was painted candy-apple red, with chrome pipes and fenders. Its red leather saddle was tricked out with silver studs. "How about this one? Perfect for running down to the grocery store on Saturday mornings."

She laughed. "I don't think so."

"Sure you don't want to give her a test-drive?"

Marlee shook her head, then walked away from him, across the garage. Her high heels clicked loudly on the concrete floor. "Are you here by yourself?" she asked.

"Wiley's up at the office. Everybody else is at lunch." She stopped in front of a Snap-on Tools calendar, her back to Troy. "This certainly brings back memories," he said. "I remember when you used to hang around the garage where I worked when we met."

"That seems like such a long time ago now." She faced him again. "I've been thinking about you and Greg. I've decided we should tell him the truth."

Her words flooded him with relief. "That's great. How do you want to handle it? I'd like us to tell him together. I can stop by tonight—"

"Hang on." She held up her hand. "School is out in ten days. We should tell him then."

"Ten days?" Troy felt much of his elation fade. "Why do we need to wait?"

"I have a few days' vacation scheduled then. That way I can spend more time with him to make sure he's okay."

"You worry too much. He'll be fine."

"You don't know that," Marlee snapped. She twisted her hands together, then spoke in a calmer voice. "We'll be able to plan exactly what to say, and to think of the right answers to questions he'll probably have."

And Marlee could prepare herself for how her own life was about to change. Troy understood that without her saying so.

"All right," he said. "We'll tell him when school is out." After six years, what was another ten days?

"Thank you."

He wanted to pull her close and promise her everything would be all right. He might have done so if the front door hadn't opened and Scotty hadn't strolled in. Clean-shaven and dressed in a new work shirt and jeans, Scotty no longer looked like a street bum, though the prison tattoos on his forearms branded him as an ex-con.

"Hey. Didn't mean to interrupt." Scotty made a move as if to exit.

"It's okay," Troy said. "Marlee, you remember Scotty. Scotty, this is Marlee."

"How do you do?" Scotty came closer and offered his hand.

Marlee shook it, though she'd gone a shade paler. "I didn't know the two of you worked together," she said.

"Yeah," Scotty said. "Small world, ain't it? Good to see you again. If you need anything, I'll be in my office." He went through a door at the far side of the shop, and shut it behind him.

Marlee frowned at Troy. "What is he doing here?" she asked.

"He's just started as a porter—cleaning up, running parts, whatever we need."

"You got him the job, didn't you?" The words were more an accusation than a question.

"I told him we needed someone."

"But he's an ex-con."

"Everyone here is. Even Wiley. It's what he does—gives jobs to guys just out of prison to help them get back on their feet."

She folded her arms over her chest. "How are you ever going to put your past behind you if you keep hanging out with other ex-cons?"

"We're not hanging out. We're working."

"It would be better if you worked somewhere else."

"And it would be great if I had a rich uncle who

died and left me ten million bucks. But that's not going to happen, any more than most places are going to hire a guy with a record. I'm lucky to have a job at all."

"Fine. But I don't want Greg exposed to any of your coworkers."

Her attitude grated. If his colleagues weren't good enough to come near their son, where did that leave Troy? She said she'd changed her mind about him, but had she really? "They're not contagious," he said. "And neither am I."

But Marlee's expression didn't soften. "I don't know them and I don't want them around my son."

"Fine. I won't invite any of them over for dinner. But if Greg wants to see where I work, I'm going to show him. And if he asks me about prison, I'm going to answer his questions as honestly as I can."

She shook her head. "That's part of your past. Why can't we try to forget it ever happened?"

"You mean lie? Tell him I was just 'away' for all these years? Where? On a mission to Mars, or stranded on a desert island?"

"I didn't say we had to lie. We can tell him you broke the law and were punished for it and it's not something we need to talk about."

"Not talking is what got us into this mess in the first place—you refusing to acknowledge me after I was arrested, so that Greg didn't even know I existed. And me not asking more questions of Raymond before I agreed to go with him the night of the robbery."

"I did what I thought was best."

"I know you did. But pretending the past never happened doesn't make it go away. It's better to be up-front and face reality. We'll both be there to help Greg cope."

"Fine." She was still clearly upset, but Troy felt he'd pushed her far enough for one afternoon. "I really have to go now," she said. She started toward the door, then stopped. "I almost forgot. Greg wanted me to invite you over Saturday. He wants us to grill burgers."

"What about you, Marlee? Do you want me to come?"

She hesitated, then nodded. "Yes. I think it would be nice." She sounded breathless, and before he could reply, she whirled around and hurried through the door.

Troy turned back to the Triumph. When would Marlee stop running away from him and run *to* him instead?

The office door opened and Scotty stepped out. "Who's Greg?" he asked.

"You were eavesdropping."

Scotty shrugged. "Good way to learn stuff. So, who's Greg?"

"Her son." *My* son. But he had to keep that secret for ten more days.

Scotty sat on a stool in one corner of the garage and lit a cigarette, then picked up a newspaper from the tool bench and began flipping through it. Troy knelt once more in front of the Triumph. Marlee was going to have to get over her fear of his past if they were ever going to be a couple again. He couldn't walk on eggshells around her, afraid to mention his past in case he upset her. And though he would never want Greg to think prison or the people in it were cool, he didn't want his son to be afraid of him, either.

"Well, what do you know," Scotty said, exhaling a cloud of smoke.

"What?" Troy glanced over his shoulder.

"Friend of mine's getting a big award from the mayor today." He pointed to an article at the bottom of the front page. "Frank Britton. Says here he saved a woman from a fire. You know him?"

"Never met the guy." Frank had been "away" while Troy and Marlee were dating.

"Think I'll go down and say hello," Scotty said. "Come with me and I'll introduce you. Frank's a great guy."

"No, thanks." Part of him *was* curious to meet the man who'd figured so large in Marlee's life, but he didn't see how any good could come of it. "I've got plenty of work to do around here."

"I guess you're right." Scotty set aside the paper. "Didn't Wiley want us to go pick up that custom trike over on Riverside this afternoon?"

"Someone needs to, yeah. You can go."

Scotty shook his head. "Wiley took the trailer with him this morning. But if you ride over there with me, you can drive the trike back here."

"Or we could wait until tomorrow when we have the trailer."

"Wiley wanted it today. Besides, it's a beautiful day. Don't you want to get out of this place for a while?"

Through the open shop door, Troy could see a patch of bright blue sky above a fringe of green trees. It was the kind of scenery he'd dreamed about when he was behind bars. He tossed the wrench he'd been holding on to the workbench. "I guess it wouldn't hurt to run over and pick up that trike," he said.

CHAPTER NINE

SCOTTY GRABBED THE KEYS and slid into the driver's seat of the old pickup Wiley kept for transporting parts. Troy buckled his seatbelt and tried to shake the feeling that Scotty was up to something. Maybe it was because he'd given in so easily when Troy had nixed the idea of visiting Frank Britton. And then he'd been so eager to run this errand....

Troy's worst suspicions were confirmed when Scotty turned, not onto Riverside Drive, but onto Fifth, headed toward the Travis County Courthouse. "What are you doing?" Troy demanded.

"I just want to stop a minute and say hi to Frank." He gunned the engine, then swerved into a parking space. He was out of the truck before Troy could grab him, and he took the keys with him.

Troy went after him and caught up with him just in time to see the mayor shake hands with a slight, older man as camera flashes exploded around them. While reporters swarmed to interview the hero of the day, Troy stopped short and studied Marlee's father.

Frank Britton was maybe five-ten, with thick gray

hair and the weathered face of a man ten years his senior. His suit was too big in the shoulders, but he stood ramrod straight, unintimidated by the mass of people around him. He smiled, revealing even white teeth Troy suspected were false, and cracked jokes with the reporters, clearly enjoying the attention.

At last the press turned away and the mayor and his staff went inside, leaving Frank on the steps, clutching a small walnut plaque and the envelope with the check that came with the award.

"Hey, Frank, congratulations." Scotty bounded up the steps and shook Frank's hand. "You remember me, don't you—Richard Scott—Scotty."

"Hey, Scotty. 'Course I remember you." Frank glanced at Troy.

"This is my pal Troy." Scotty clapped Troy on the shoulder. "He wanted to meet you."

Troy glared at Scotty. The little weasel would pay for this, he silently promised. He realized Frank was waiting for him to say something. "Congratulations," he said.

Frank admired the plaque. "Yeah, this was pretty nice. I never expected it, of course. I just did what any right-thinking person would."

Troy had the feeling Frank had said these words a hundred times since the fire. They rolled off his tongue with an ease that could only come from repetition.

"So what you up to these days?" Scotty asked as the three men descended the courthouse steps and started down the sidewalk.

"Nothing much," Frank said.

Scotty lowered his voice. "You got anything going on? I could use the work," he said.

"You have a job," Troy said.

"You know what I mean." Scotty turned to Frank. "I'm cleaning up at the motorcycle shop where Troy's a mechanic, but I'm always on the lookout for a better-paying gig."

"I'm retired," Frank said, staring straight ahead.

"It's okay," Scotty said. "You can talk around Troy. He's been inside." He put his hand on the older man's shoulder. "Let's go get a beer and talk about it."

"Leave me out of this." Troy grabbed the truck keys from Scotty's hand and took a step back.

"Come on, man," Scotty said. "Don't tell me you couldn't use some extra cash. I'll bet Frank knows where we could get it."

Troy shook his head. "I've got too much at stake to screw up again."

"That's right," Scotty said. "Troy has a girl. A real cutie."

"That's nice," Frank said. "What's her name?"

Troy couldn't betray Marlee that way. "No one you know," he said, and walked away.

He was almost back at the truck when a familiar figure intercepted him. "Hello, Troy," Bernie said.

"Hey, Bernie." Troy took out his keys and jingled them nervously in his hand.

The parole officer glanced over Troy's shoulder. "You didn't take my advice about staying away from Frank Britton," he said.

"It wasn't my idea to come here," Troy said.

"I saw you with him and Scotty. What were the three of you talking about?"

"Nothing."

Bernie waited, arms folded across his chest, as if he expected Troy to elaborate.

Troy waited, too. The less he said, the less Bernie could twist his words. Finally, Bernie broke the silence. "I'm keeping an eye on you," he said.

"I'm not doing anything illegal," Troy said.

"You're hanging out with the wrong people. Isn't that what got you into trouble before?"

What could Troy say to that? Seven years behind bars made it hard to maintain friendships with those outside. Other than Marlee and a few coworkers, the only people he knew were men he'd done time with. Was that why it was so hard for cons to get away from the life?

Maybe for other men, but Troy was determined to do it. "I'm not going to screw up, Bernie," he said.

Bernie nodded. "See that you don't. You might not believe it, but I'm on your side here." He jerked his head in the direction of the two men Troy had left behind. "I don't want to see you end up like Frank. He's a hero today, but he still has a rap sheet as long as my arm—the kind of record he can't escape. You've got a chance to make a different kind of life."

"And I will." Troy climbed into the truck and started the engine. All the plaques and citations in the world couldn't make up for the hurt Frank had caused his family. Troy would do anything to keep from making the same mistakes.

MARLEE STOOD in the doorway and watched Troy flipping burgers at the grill. From this position she had a good view of his butt, the softly faded denim of his jeans clinging just so. She wondered what he'd do if she slipped her hand into his back pocket, the way she used to when they were dating.

"What are you smiling about?" he asked, looking over his shoulder with a smile of his own.

"Was I smiling?" She pretended nonchalance, willing her face not to heat.

"I thought maybe you liked what you saw."

She glanced toward Greg, who was busy excavating his sandbox with the toy dump truck Troy had given him. "Can't blame a woman for looking," she said, deciding to be bold.

The lines at the corners of his eyes deepened as he grinned. "I don't mind you looking. Or touching."

Oh, she knew how he felt about her. He'd made it perfectly clear. But she wasn't the kind of woman who would have sex for the sake of sex, no matter how lonely she was.

Not that Troy wanted that, either. His dream was for them to be a family—husband and wife and child. The audacity of such a commitment took her breath away. He apparently expected all or nothing from her; the prospect was too daunting to consider. "How are those burgers doing?" she asked.

"They need a few more minutes." He lowered the cover on the grill and faced her.

"Mom! Troy! Come look at what I made."

Unsure if she was grateful or sorry for the interruption, Marlee went to kneel beside Greg in the sandbox. Troy joined her on Greg's other side.

"It's a fort, see?" Greg indicated the packed sand walls. A row of plastic soldiers took aim from behind the wall at more soldiers positioned amid sand dunes.

"That's great." Troy picked up one of the soldiers from behind the dunes and aimed him toward the fort. *"Pow, pow, pow."*

Greg grabbed a soldier from the fort. *"Pow, pow. I got you!"*

"Ooohh! I'm done for." Troy's soldier writhed in agony, then fell backward in the sand.

The soldiers had been a gift from Troy, also. Marlee had been determined to give her child only nonsexist, nonviolent toys, though she'd admitted it was a lost cause the first time Greg had turned a stick into a make-believe weapon.

For the next few minutes, the battle raged, Troy and Greg taking turns acting out dramatic death scenes. One of Troy's men made a sneak attack on the fort, only to be thrown from the high walls. Greg's men made sensational leaps to their own deaths whenever Troy's aim was true.

When all the plastic men lay scattered in the sand, Greg grinned up at Troy. "This is fun," he said. "I never had a grown-up play with me like this before."

"I play with you!" Marlee protested.

"Yeah, but you never want to play soldiers or cowboys or anything like that. You know—guy stuff."

Marlee laughed, and tousled his hair. Troy's eyes met hers and she felt a small surge of gratitude toward him. Greg needed his father, and she was pleased Troy could be there for him. There were things he and Troy could share that Marlee could never understand. Now that she trusted Troy more, she could admit that that was all right. If only she could believe that Troy's past would never come back to hurt Greg.

"I bet those burgers are about ready." Troy stood and helped Marlee up out of the sand. "Want to hold the plate while I take them off the grill?" he asked Greg.

"Yeah!"

"I'll get the buns and potato salad," Marlee said, heading into the house.

She returned a moment later with the food, just as Troy scooped Greg up under his arm. "Put me down!" Greg giggled as Troy carried him to the picnic table.

Marlee put her hands on her hips and gave them a mock frown. "All right, *children,* settle down."

"Yes, ma'am." Troy slid onto the bench next to her and winked at Greg. The boy winked in return, then turned to Marlee and winked again. It was something he'd just learned to do—another gift from Troy, she suspected.

"It looks delicious," Troy said as he slathered mustard on his burger.

"Mom makes the best burgers," Greg said. "And you did a good job of cooking them."

"We make a pretty great team, then," Troy said.

It had been ages since Marlee had thought of herself as part of a team. She couldn't decide if she liked the idea or not. Two people working together could accomplish more, but how could you ever be sure the other person had the same goals as you? How could you ever really know another person as well as you knew yourself?

AFTER SUPPER, Greg insisted on challenging Troy and Marlee to a game of lawn darts. The boys team of Troy and Greg narrowly defeated Marlee in a loud, fast-paced game with oversize darts tossed at a target on the grass that left them all laughing and exhausted. Afterward, they collapsed into lawn chairs and gazed up at the stars. Troy held Greg on his lap and pointed out the Big Dipper and the Milky Way. "How'd you learn so much about the stars?" Greg asked.

"My father taught me when I was little."

"Mine did, too." Marlee said the words so quietly, she might have been speaking to herself.

"How old were you?" Troy asked.

She looked down and smoothed the fraying cuff of her shorts. "Five or six, I guess. It would have been before…" She glanced at Greg, who was leaning back against Troy's chest, still staring up at the stars. "Before he went away the first time."

"I bet you missed him," Troy said softly.

She nodded. "I didn't know then where he was…or why." Her voice was reedy, her anguish evident even after twenty years.

"When did you find out?"

She looked at Greg again. Troy felt the boy's deep, steady breathing and wondered if he'd fallen asleep. He watched Marlee out of the corner of his eye, suppressing the urge to stroke her hair. If he touched her, she might retreat, the closeness between them destroyed.

"I was ten. My aunt took me to see him." Anger edged the soft tones of her words. "She thought I should know."

Troy gripped the metal arms of the lawn chair with one hand until his knuckles whitened. "Did she at least warn you first?"

Marlee bit her lip and shook her head. Troy thought he saw the glimmer of tears, but she looked away. The only sound that broke the silence was the gentle cadence of Greg's breathing as he slept in Troy's lap.

"It was an awful place," Marlee said after a long while. "When they brought him out, he didn't look like himself. At home he always dressed so neatly, in the latest styles. He always wore flashy suits and alligator shoes. I thought of him as young and handsome and funny. There he looked…old and ugly and…and sad." The last word was barely audible, but it echoed in Troy's head with all the things she didn't need to say.

Her father would have come into the visitors' room in shackles, wearing baggy prison coveralls, his hair cut short in no particular style, rubber sandals on his feet. Everyone would have stared at him—the guards and the other prisoners and the self-righteous woman who had taken it upon herself to destroy a little girl's illusions. And the little girl herself would have stared in horror at the man and the place, while her heart shattered like glass.

Troy reached out to lay his hand on Marlee's in a gesture of comfort, but she pulled away and sat upright. "I think Greg's asleep," she said with exaggerated calm. "I'd better put him to bed."

"Let me." He cradled the boy gently in his arms and stood. "Please."

She hesitated, then nodded. "All right. His pajamas are in the top dresser drawer."

"Don't worry. I'll find everything."

Greg hardly stirred as Troy got him changed into pajamas printed with images of the Tasmanian Devil. He tucked the covers around him and kissed him on the forehead, lingering to breathe in the little-boy smell of sandbox and burgers. Then he switched off the light and tiptoed from the room, feeling blessed by those tender moments with his son.

When he returned to the living room, Marlee was sitting on the sofa. Troy sat beside her. "I don't think he woke up once," he said.

She smiled. "He goes and goes until he can't go anymore, then falls right to sleep. I envy that sometimes."

"I once heard that the difference between kids and adults is that kids hate to nap, while adults wish they could."

"I guess so. When I was little, I thought being an

adult meant you could stay up as late as you wanted and you could smoke cigarettes. Now I don't care about either one."

"So your parents smoked when you were growing up?"

"Yes. So did all their friends. I thought it was very glamorous, though I see it differently now. I guess I saw a lot of things differently as I got older."

"I never knew anything about your dad," he said. "Thanks for telling me some of it now." Marlee had never hidden her contempt for the old man, or her shame that he'd spent most of her life in and out of jail. But today was the first time he'd glimpsed another side of their relationship. Marlee had loved her father once; she apparently still grieved over losing him.

"I don't think about him much," she said. "It's just too sad."

"I saw Frank Wednesday afternoon," he said. "I didn't tell you before because I didn't want to upset you."

"You saw him?" She stared at him. "Where?"

"He received an award from the mayor—for rescuing that woman from the fire. I was downtown and caught the end of the ceremony."

"Did you say anything to him?"

"Scotty introduced me. Apparently they know each other."

"From prison, I'm sure."

"My parole officer was there, too. He said Frank's been straight about five years now." There was no need to tell Marlee that Bernie hadn't actually said that *then*.

"Well, good for him." Her voice was sharp with sarcasm.

"I take it he's never tried to contact you?"

"No. I made it clear I never wanted to see him again."

One more thing Troy and Frank didn't have in common—Troy hadn't taken Marlee's refusal for an answer.

"You didn't say anything to him about me, did you?" she asked.

"Of course not. We hardly said three words."

"Why did you even go there?"

"It was Scotty's idea. But I admit I was curious to see him. After all, he's part of who you are."

"He's part of who I *was*. Not who I am now."

"Right." But could one be separated from the other?

Marlee tucked her legs under her and shifted to face him. "Tell me about the night you were arrested," she said. "Not what came out in court, but the full story."

"You really want to know?" Troy studied her face, trying to read her motives. Was she searching for reasons to resist the growing attraction between them? Or was she trying to justify letting him get closer?

"I don't know if you ever met my cousin, Raymond. He lived in Round Rock and was a little older than me. He always seemed to have plenty of money, so when I found out you were pregnant, I decided to ask if he'd give me a loan. I wanted extra cash for the baby and to pay for a wedding. I figured I'd pick up some more hours at the garage and pay him back."

Troy fixed his gaze on a pile of magazines on the coffee table, but as he continued his story, his vision blurred. He could see the events of that day too clearly...

He'd met Raymond at the old Night Hawk restaurant downtown, to talk about the loan. His cousin had been wearing Levi's and a collarless white shirt, snakeskin boots and a designer leather jacket. He'd looked like a movie star. Troy, in his faded Wranglers, T-shirt and work boots, had felt like a hick as he slid into the booth across from his cousin.

"So you're thinking about tying the knot." Raymond grinned at him. "This calls for a celebration. How about coming with me to Fredricksburg this evening?"

"Fredricksburg?" Troy shifted nervously in the booth.

"Sure. We'll have a few drinks and celebrate. You can help me with a little job I've got down there and when we get back I'll give you all the money you need."

Troy cleared his throat. "I'd appreciate the loan, Ray."

Raymond waved his hand. "No loan, cuz. We'll just call it payment for you helping me out tonight."

"Uh, what kind of job is it?"

Raymond smiled. "Nothing much. Shouldn't take more than a few minutes."

All the money he needed for a few minutes' work. He and Marlee and the baby would be able to get off to a good start. Troy knew it shouldn't be this easy, but he shrugged off the shiver of unease that ran up his spine. He nodded. "Sure. I'll help you out."

Raymond insisted they go right then, leaving Troy's motorcycle in the parking lot and setting out in Raymond's Crown Victoria. They stopped at a club on the outskirts of San Marcos and Raymond ordered drink after drink, though Troy was too nervous to have more than a couple of beers. Once he asked Raymond about the mysterious job, but his cousin waved him off. "You'll find out soon enough," he said. It was after midnight when they set out again, Troy driving and following Raymond's directions.

"Pull in here a minute while I run in and get us some more beer." Raymond pointed out a convenience store and Troy swung the car into the parking lot.

He left the engine running while Raymond went inside. The green neon of the store's marquee bathed the car's interior with an underwater glow. Troy fiddled with the dial of the radio and thought about Marlee. He should have called her from the club, just to say good-night. They talked every evening and she'd be wondering why she hadn't heard anything.

He heard a sound like a truck backfiring and looked up. The car shook as Raymond jerked open the door. "Let's get the hell out of here!" he said as he slid into the seat. He dropped a brown paper bag on the floor between his feet. Troy heard coins rattle against beer bottles.

"What's the rush?" he asked, putting the car in gear.

"I just robbed the place." Raymond's eyes were wild, his breath hot and smelling of whiskey. The hair on the back of Troy's neck rose as he stared at the pistol hanging loose in Raymond's right hand. "Step on it!" his cousin shouted.

Troy swore and stomped on the gas, tires squealing as the car jolted over the curb and into the street. "You're crazy!" he said as he rushed a yellow light and headed toward the interstate.

Raymond laughed and reached into the bag at his feet. He pulled out two beers and a handful of bills. "There's your wedding present, cousin," he said, tossing the money into Troy's lap. He twisted off the caps on the beer and shoved one toward Troy. "Congratulations."

Troy slapped the beer away and gripped the steering wheel until his knuckles ached. "How could you be so stupid?" he barked at his cousin.

"You're the one who's stupid." Raymond pointed the gun at him and laughed. "Sweating for a living when there's an easier way."

Troy ignored him. He wanted nothing to do with Raymond or his money ever again. He'd provide for Marlee and the baby honestly, no matter how much overtime he had to work.

Lights flashed in the rearview mirror and he

heard a siren's piercing whine. Raymond swore. He rolled down the window and hurled the gun out into the night. "Floor it!" he shouted. "We can outrun them."

Fear overruled commonsense. Troy stomped on the gas and the car swerved. Raymond was thrown into the dash, swearing loudly. Troy fought to control the fishtailing car, but couldn't when he heard gunshots and one tire suddenly blew—shot out by the cops following them. Skidding wildly, he somehow steered the car to the shoulder.

The next few moments were a blur. Cops were everywhere, shouting at them to come out with their hands up. Troy remembered lying facedown by the side of the road, the smell of tar and diesel engulfing him, gravel digging into one cheek. A two-hundred-pound officer had his knee in Troy's back and was shouting at him as he cuffed him.

Troy tried to explain what had happened, but the cops ordered him to be quiet. They took him and Raymond to the police station in separate cars, and he spent a sleepless night in a concrete cell. During his interrogation, Troy learned that Raymond had shot the clerk at the store.

Despite the efforts of his court-appointed attorney, no one believed he was innocent. Not the cops, the jury or the judge who sentenced him to twelve years in the Texas State Penitentiary for armed robbery.

"I couldn't believe I'd been so stupid," Troy said now, staring at the carpet beneath his feet.

Marlee put her hand on his back. He took comfort

in that one small gesture. "I'm sorry," she said. "Sorry for not answering your letters, and for not believing in your innocence."

"I was guilty, all right. I did drive the car, and I did try to evade the police. But mostly, I was guilty of being stupid."

"You trusted the wrong person," she said. "That's all."

Troy turned toward her, and she pulled him into an embrace that squeezed out much of the pain and fear that had lingered since that long-ago night with his cousin.

He kissed her neck, the skin soft as satin and smelling of almonds. One kiss led to a dozen, and then a dozen more. She let out a low sigh, and sagged against him.

He brought his hands up to cup the soft swell of her breasts. Her nipples hardened at his touch, pressing into his palms. She leaned her head against his shoulder. "Don't stop," she whispered.

"I won't." He stroked her through the fabric.

She moaned, and he tilted her head up to his, then kissed her, a long, deep kiss that told her how he felt better than words. He wanted to remind her of all the ways they had loved each other before, and could love again.

She responded ardently, stroking his back and making small, murmuring sounds that encouraged him.

He urged her to lie down on the sofa, and started to stretch out beside her, but as he did, he bumped the coffee table, overturning a candlestick, sending the candle rolling.

They both jerked, startled. Marlee stared at him, dazed. "What was that?"

"It's just a candlestick. It's all right." He started to kiss her again, but she pushed him away.

"We'd better stop," she said.

Understanding dawned. "You're worried about Greg, aren't you? Hey, it's okay. He's out like a light. He won't hear a thing. Or we could go into your bedroom and lock the door."

She shook her head. "It's not that. Or not *only* that. It's— I'm not ready for this."

Whereas he'd been ready for months. Maybe years. But he didn't want Marlee for just one night. He wanted the kind of love that lasted a lifetime, and he could wait for her to come to him.

"Have dinner with me tomorrow," he said. "Just the two of us."

"You mean…like a date?"

"Yeah. A date." He'd proved he could be a good father, now he would show her he could be a good partner to her as well.

She looked doubtful. "I don't think I can get a sitter on such short notice."

"I'll find a sitter. Someone you'll like. I promise."

She worried her lower lip between her teeth. He held his breath. Finally, she nodded. "All right. But I think you should go now."

"All right. I'll see you tomorrow." He got up from the couch and kissed her on the forehead, then turned and headed for the door. He had a lot to do before tomorrow night. Everything had to be perfect. The rest of his life depended on it.

CHAPTER TEN

MARLEE PACED back and forth across her bedroom floor the following evening, unable to settle down for a moment as she dressed. Were these earrings all right? Maybe she should wear her red blouse instead of the purple. Where were her shoes?

"You look pretty, Mom." Greg strolled into the room and plopped onto the bed.

Marlee paused and stared at him. She didn't have to ask where he'd acquired that tough-guy swagger or nonchalant tone of voice. It was the same place he'd learned his new way of standing, thumbs tucked into his belt loops, one hip cocked. Had he spent hours practicing in front of the mirror? Or had these new mannerisms surfaced naturally, heredity in action?

The doorbell rang and she jumped. "I'll get it!" Greg shouted and raced past her.

She followed slowly down the hall, ignoring the furious pounding of her heart. *It's only dinner,* she told herself.

Dinner with Troy. Alone. And what would they do after dinner? They'd come so close to making love the night before. Tonight, with no interruptions, no child sleeping in the next room, would she finally surrender to temptation?

She turned the corner and almost ran into Trish, who was coming out of the living room, carrying a grocery sack. "Trish, what are you doing here?" Marlee asked, confused.

"Surprise!" Trish held up one arm. "I'm here to look after the G-man while you and Troy go out." She opened her bag. "See, I came prepared. I've got videos, puzzle books, popcorn..."

"I told you I'd get somebody nice."

Marlee looked up and saw Troy sauntering toward them. She drew in her breath, struck dumb by the sight of him in a black leather jacket and biker's chaps over black jeans. Even his shirt was black, and looked so soft her fingers itched to touch it.

"Talk about tall, dark and handsome," Trish whispered in Marlee's ear. "My roommate just about dropped her teeth when she answered the door and found him standing there."

"What are you two whispering about?" Troy halted in front of them. Greg stopped beside him. The little boy ran his hand up and down the leather chaps. Marlee's knees felt weak as she wished she could do the same.

"Wouldn't you like to know?" Trish teased.

"You look great, as always," Troy said, smiling at Marlee.

She smoothed her hand down the front of her short, full skirt. The skirt was black, setting off her purple silk blouse. She liked how the combination made her feel, but now, judging by the way Troy was looking at her, she wondered if the outfit wasn't too revealing, showing too much leg, the blouse clinging too tightly. But then, Troy wouldn't need much imagination—at one time he'd known her body as well as his own. The thought sent a quiver through her stomach.

She knelt and drew Greg to her in a hug. "You be good and mind Trish, okay?"

He squirmed and nodded. "All right, Mom." He looked up at Troy, obviously embarrassed. "Why do girls have to get so mushy?"

"Oh, I don't know. When you get older, you might not think it's so bad." Troy chuckled and held out his hand. "Put her there, partner."

Marlee released her son so he could exchange high fives with Troy. A few last-minute instructions to Trish and they were out the door.

Troy's motorcycle sat in the driveway, the chrome shining in the glow of the porch light. He picked up a bright red helmet and handed it to her. "Put this on."

He helped her adjust the chin strap, then donned his own helmet and lowered the visor. "I remember when you used to ride behind me on my old bike," he said.

The engine rumbled to life and a corresponding tremor shot through her. "Climb on," he said, his voice raised over the steady throb of the engine. "Use the footrests there and hold on tight."

She gripped the seat beneath her and stared at Troy's broad back as he guided the bike down the driveway. He negotiated the turn onto the street and sped forward. Instinctively, Marlee reached for the only handhold in sight—Troy. She pressed her cheek into his jacket, closing her eyes against the dizzying sight of the street disappearing under the wheels.

He turned onto the highway, toward the lake. As she adjusted to the sensation of speed and open air, Marlee began to relax. She eased her constricting hold on Troy and raised her head to look around, though she still kept her arms securely around him.

She'd forgotten how exhilarating this could be. The world looked different from a motorcycle— closer, not shut off by protective metal and glass the way it was from a car. She noticed sights she'd never seen before, like graffiti on a bridge railing, and the almost fluorescent yellow and purple of wildflowers growing below lighted billboards.

The sensation of holding Troy so close distracted her, yet he seemed oblivious, his attention on guiding the bike. They drove along the lake, past marinas and dry docks, up a narrow street to a small park beside the water. Marlee felt a catch in her throat as she recognized their destination. She and Troy had spent many an evening in each other's arms in this secret hideaway.

He parked and shut off the engine. The silence closed in around them. Gradually, she made out the sound of water lapping against the shore, and the hum of the mercury-vapor light at the tackle shop. "Why did you bring me here?" she asked.

"We needed someplace private to talk." He swung his leg over the bike and climbed off. "I brought dinner. Why don't we eat first."

She dismounted and watched Troy unpack a small cooler and a quilt from the saddlebags. He threw the quilt over one shoulder, then headed into the trees.

She followed him, ducking under low branches, feeling almost as if she were walking back in time as she made her way along the narrow path.

The path opened onto a clearing, twenty yards or so across. A picnic table sat on a swath of green grass beside the water, shielded from the rest of the park by trees. A full moon bathed the area in a silver glow.

He spread the quilt over the table. "I stopped by the Central Market on my way to your house."

Marlee stared at the feast Troy placed before her. The food looked delicious—filled bites of puff pastry, stuffed mushrooms, cheese, fresh strawberries, chocolate. Exotic, sensuous food. Food for lovers to feed each other.

"I wasn't sure what you'd want, so I got a little bit of everything." He met her eyes expectantly.

"It…it all looks delicious."

"Yeah, well, better than what we used to eat here." He chuckled.

She thought his laughter sounded forced. Was he thinking the same thing she was—that what they'd eaten had never mattered? The French fries and cheeseburgers had only provided the energy to satisfy the more insistent hunger between them.

"Why don't I pour the drinks." He twisted the cap on a bottle of soda, then filled a pair of plastic cups. "Not very elegant, I'm afraid." His voice was steady, but his hand shook as he handed her the cup.

She sipped the drink, the carbonation tickling her nose. Troy settled onto the other end of the picnic bench.

Alone with him in such an intimate setting—one that brought back so many memories—Marlee wasn't sure how to act. She told herself she'd have been nervous on any first date. But with Troy, every interaction was complicated by knowledge of what they'd had before, and all that had happened since. Her feelings for Troy were more complicated, as well. This wasn't the Troy of their youth, but a more serious, determined man who had touched her heart and soul.

"These mushrooms look wonderful." She popped the hors d'oeuvre into her mouth. "Mmm. I wonder what kind of seasoning they use." The mushroom might have been seasoned with sawdust for all she could taste it.

Troy shifted on the bench. "Seasoning? Uh...I don't know. I just picked up a few things so we could eat in private."

Private. Alone. Where they were free to do almost anything.... She drained the rest of the soda from her cup. "Wow. I was thirsty. Would you pour me some more?"

"Marlee, why are you so nervous?"

"N-nervous?" She leaned away from him, one hand going involuntarily to her throat. She felt naked beneath his gaze.

He slid across the bench toward her. "What are you afraid of?" he asked, his voice a velvet growl.

"I'm not afraid." She leaned farther back, holding her breath and staring into his eyes, mesmerized.

"Are you afraid I brought you here to seduce you?" He bent over her, his powerful body covering her, surrounding her. "You know I want you, don't you?" He trailed one hand along her cheek, his touch as gentle as a feather, but with the possibility of power and strength. "Do you want to leave?"

"No." The word was a gasp. As she said it, she closed her eyes, and felt him pull her into his arms.

She sighed as his mouth covered hers, his kiss insistent, searching. He swept his tongue inside her mouth, tasting, teasing, tantalizing her with promises of the delight that could be hers.

Her fear evaporated, replaced by a hot urgency. She gripped the front of his jacket, letting the teeth of the zipper bite into her palms. She wanted to merge her body with his and never let go.

He resisted her grasp, moving away and holding her at arm's length. The seductive look he gave her made her squirm in frustration. "We've waited so long already," he said, his voice rough with desire. He kissed her gently on the forehead. "But I won't rush. I want to make it right for you...so right."

He caressed her with his gaze, telling her how much he wanted her, needed her. Eyes locked on hers, he freed her blouse from her skirt and eased his hand up her side. He stroked her ribs, sending delicious tremors through her, then cupped her breast in his palm. The heat of his touch burned away her last hesitation.

She let her head fall back. "Don't stop," she

breathed. "Please, don't stop." With the cool night air around her and the moonlit sky overhead, Marlee felt wild and wanton, like a teenager again, but with a woman's knowledge of life to deepen her lust.

But Troy did stop, one hand covering her breast, the other at her back, supporting her. "Marlee, we can't do this here," he said.

She blinked, bringing her surroundings into focus. This was a public park and they were adults, no longer irresponsible teenagers. "We could go to your place," she said.

He shook his head. "My place is a mess—a typical bachelor pad." He stroked her cheek with the back of his hand. "You deserve better."

She thought of her own bed, so clean and comfortable…but Trish and Greg were there. "We could get a room somewhere," she said.

Hope brightened the desire in his eyes. "If you're sure…"

"I'm sure." She stood and began gathering up the picnic. "Come on."

They didn't speak on the ride to a hotel on the lake.

She waited with the bike while Troy checked in and returned to her with the room key. Though she couldn't imagine eating, they carried the picnic into the elevator with them. They stood on opposite sides of the car, watching the numbers light up as they rode to the fourteenth floor. They were careful not to touch, as if aware that to do so would break down their last inhibitions.

Only when they were safely inside the room, with the lights on and door locked, did she turn to Troy.

"This was a good idea," he said. "Much better than my place."

"Shh." She put two fingers to his lips. "Kiss me," she whispered.

There was nothing gentle about the way Troy crushed his mouth to hers, but the ferocity of the caress matched her need for him. She rose on her toes, straining to be even closer, and they tugged at each other's clothes.

They fell upon the bed, still half-dressed, and lay facing each other. He ran one finger under the edge of her bra, his rough skin snagging on the smooth satin. She quivered at the first stroking touch of his finger, and pressed against him, wanting so much more.

He lifted his head. "Look at me," he whispered.

Marlee opened her eyes and his gaze stripped her emotions of all pretense, laying them bare. The intensity of his expression made her shiver with desire.

He began to lavish kisses along her jaw, down her neck, across her shoulders. He unbuttoned her blouse and blazed a path to the top of her breast, then continued across the fabric, suckling her hard, aching nipple through the satin.

She moaned at the contact, writhing beneath him as he transferred his attention from one breast to the other.

"I've dreamed about this for seven years," he murmured as he unfastened her bra. "Sometimes I thought I'd go crazy from wanting you so much." He began to lick and suckle each naked breast in turn until she thought *she'd* go mad with longing.

He smiled at her, full of the knowledge of his power over her, then he edged one finger up her leg, to the aching juncture of her thighs. She arched toward him, urging him closer.

He stopped and moved away. She whimpered and reached for him. "Hush," he soothed. He unzipped his pants, then pulled a package from his pocket. "I'm not going away." He tossed the condom onto the night-stand, then leaned over to help her out of her panties.

He bent his head and kissed her curls, his tongue finding the center of her desire and coaxing her to the brink. She was panting now, reaching for that wonderful height.

He stopped and raised his head. "Say you want me," he said.

"Wh-what?"

He slid up her body, bringing his face close to hers. "I want to hear you say it. Say you want me."

She stared at him, at his passion-darkened eyes, his mouth wet with her own arousal. She had never wanted anyone more. "I want you," she breathed.

He kneeled between her legs and sheathed himself in the condom. Then he was filling her, stroking her, driving her to the edge.

TROY WATCHED the play of emotion on Marlee's face and felt a storm of feeling he struggled to control. So many dark nights and lonely mornings the memory of their lovemaking had tortured him. To have another chance to love her was too sweet a blessing to take in.

His passion threatened to overwhelm him, but he forced himself to wait for her, as she'd waited for him all these years.

He coaxed her toward her climax, felt her muscles tense, then throb with the strength of her release. Closing his eyes, he abandoned himself to his own driving need. He came powerfully, emptying himself completely.

Eyes shut tight, he pulled her close and rolled onto his side. She wrapped one leg around him as if to keep him near. He kissed her ear. "Don't worry. I won't ever leave you again," he whispered.

"I won't *let* you leave."

He stroked her back, waiting for his heartbeat to return to normal.

She snuggled closer and chuckled softly.

"What are you laughing about?" he asked.

"Before, I was so nervous…and excited, I couldn't eat. Now I'm starving."

"Oh, you are, are you?" He pushed himself out of bed and crossed the room, naked, aware of her gaze on him. He quickly filled a plate from their picnic leftovers and brought it to her.

"Thank you." She sat up and went to take the plate, but he held it out of her reach and settled beside her.

"Allow me." He selected a mushroom and put it to her lips. She took a bite, juices running down his fingers.

"Have some cheese," she said, offering him a square of cheddar.

He laughed and captured the cheese in his mouth, along with the tips of her fingers. Her eyes flared as he suckled her fingertips.

They fed each other strawberries and chocolate and drank from the same glass. Then they lay back on the bed and made love again, more slowly this time, lingering over each other's bodies.

Troy ran his fingers along the barely visible white lines across Marlee's abdomen. "Are these from the baby?"

She nodded and made a face. "I've got varicose veins, too."

He trailed his hand to her breast. They were fuller than he remembered, the nipples more prominent. A woman's breasts instead of a girl's. "Did you nurse him?"

She nodded. "That was my favorite part of having a baby."

He imagined her with an infant at her breast, a brown-haired Madonna holding his child. "I'm sure you were beautiful." He didn't add that he wished he could've been with her. He leaned over and kissed her. "You'll always be beautiful to me."

They didn't speak after that, all their attention on physical pleasure. They moved by instinct and memory, each knowing what would please the other most. This time when Troy climaxed, he felt like a man reaching the end of a long journey.

After a while, Marlee moved out of his arms and began to put on her clothes. He dressed, too, and packed the remains of their supper. He started to open the door, but she stopped him with a hand on his arm. "One more kiss," she said.

She tasted of wine and chocolate and sex, and smelled of musk and perfume and the starch from the sheets on which they'd lain. Troy crushed her to him, lingering over the kiss as if it was the last one he'd ever know.

But of course it wouldn't be the last. Soon he hoped they would spend every night together.

Buoyed by this prospect, he raced the bike out of the garage. Marlee tightened her arms around him and he smiled. Had he ever been happier than he was right now? The things that mattered most to him— Marlee and Greg—were within his reach once more. The thought made him feel like flying. He twisted the throttle and the engine roared. They shot forward at breathtaking speed. Marlee gripped him tighter and they raced into the night.

His exhilaration vanished as red, blue and white lights flashed in his mirrors, and he heard a siren above the roar of the engine. His heart slammed in his chest and sweat prickled his palms. He swore as he steered the bike toward the shoulder.

MARLEE LOOKED BACK at the patrol car pulling in behind them and bit back a groan.

The window of the patrol car rolled down and the cop leaned out. "Put your kickstand down, turn off the engine and remove your keys from the ignition," he instructed.

Troy had the bike stopped and the kickstand down

before the cop finished speaking. Marlee watched in amazement as he jerked the keys from the ignition and dropped them on the ground. They lay on the shoulder, glinting in the flashing lights of the patrol car.

Troy left his hand outstretched, palm open. His body was rigid; Marlee could feel the tension in every muscle.

The officer walked toward them, his boots crunching in the gravel. He stopped beside the motorcycle and played the beam of a flashlight over them. He nodded politely. "Evening, sir. I need to see your license, registration and proof of insurance, please. I'll need some ID for you, too, ma'am."

"It's in my wallet, Officer," Troy said. "Just inside my jacket here." He moved with exaggerated slowness, carefully pulling the wallet from his jacket and opening it where the cop could see it. Marlee took her license from her purse and handed it to the officer.

The officer examined the licenses and other paperwork. "Any particular reason you were driving so fast?" he asked, his manner easygoing, affable. Marlee began to relax, too.

But Troy remained absolutely still. He continued to stare at the pavement. "No, sir."

"I clocked you at seventy-five back at 2222 and Mount Bonnell. The speed limit is fifty-five."

"Yes, sir."

"I'll be right with you." The cop returned to his patrol car.

Marlee heard the muffled squawk of the radio

over the whine of a semitruck approaching, then passing them. The biting odor of diesel fumes filled her nostrils in the truck's wake. "Rotten luck, huh?" she said, patting Troy's shoulder.

He didn't answer, didn't even move.

"Troy?" She leaned closer. "What's wrong?"

"Don't…say…anything." The words were strained, spoken through clenched teeth.

Marlee stared at his rigid back. She wished he would turn and look at her, but he refused to lift his gaze. If she didn't know better, she might even think he was…afraid.

No. That couldn't be it. Troy was no coward.

What was taking that cop so long? She glanced behind her and saw that he was still sitting in the patrol car, talking over the radio.

"Don't turn around."

Troy's voice was low, urgent.

"What?"

"Don't turn around. Don't look at him. Do whatever he asks, don't say anything, and we'll get out of this."

She frowned. "Troy, it's just a speeding ticket."

"Just do as I ask…please."

She was about to question him further, when another patrol car pulled in behind the first. Marlee disregarded Troy's instructions and half turned in her seat as the second officer got out of his car. Together, he and the first officer approached the motorcycle. The first officer came forward while the second waited a few steps back, one hand resting on the butt of his gun. A shiver of fear crept over Marlee.

The officer's easygoing attitude had vanished. He regarded them warily, his expression stern. "Where are you headed in such a hurry?" he asked.

"I was taking the lady home, sir."

"And from there?"

"I was going to my apartment—5303A West Bend Ridge. Apartment 64D."

The officer checked the address against the license. "Are you working?"

"Yes, sir. Wiley's Custom Cycles. It's out on South First."

"I know where it is. What are you doing out this time of night?"

Marlee cringed. This was the reality of life with a record. What would be a simple traffic stop for anyone else became a demoralizing ordeal.

Troy remained stoic. "We were out at the lake, sir."

"Doing what?"

"We…we had a picnic, sir."

"A picnic. At night?" The flashlight shone in Marlee's face. She blushed in spite of herself.

"Yes, sir," Troy answered.

"Do you have any proof of that?"

"The leftovers are in the cooler there on the back."

The officer looked at the cooler, and Marlee wondered if he would demand to examine the contents. She could prove easily enough they'd been at the hotel, but Troy hadn't mentioned that. He was obviously trying to protect her, but from what?

Finally, the cop shoved his clipboard at Troy. "Sign at the bottom." He fixed Troy with a stern gaze as he passed him a copy of the signed ticket. "You can go now, but I'll be keeping my eye out for you."

"Yes, *sir.*" Marlee heard the underlying current of anger in Troy's voice, like steam escaping from a simmering kettle. The cop's expression hardened, but he said nothing. He stepped back and the two officers waited while Troy scooped his keys off the ground, then started the engine.

She sagged against his back, clinging to him as he eased the bike into traffic. "What was that all about?" she asked.

"It's because I've got a record," he said.

Marlee felt cold and queasy. Was this what life would always be like for them, the mistakes of the past returning over and over to mar the present? "But…you completed your sentence. You haven't done anything wrong."

"I'm still on parole and speeding is breaking the law. He could have taken me to jail for that ticket if he'd wanted. If you hadn't been with me, he probably would have."

She gripped him tightly, fear and sadness almost overwhelming her.

They were silent the rest of the way home. Though Marlee couldn't see Troy's face, she sensed a change in him. She no longer felt the connection they'd forged earlier in the evening. He'd withdrawn into himself, cutting her off.

Trish met them at the door of Marlee's house. "Did you two have a good time?"

Marlee forced a cheerful smile. "It was great. Thanks so much for watching Greg." She walked past Trish, into the house. "I hope he didn't give you any trouble."

"Of course not. He's an absolute angel." She followed Marlee into the living room. "So you had fun. Where did you go?"

"It's late. I'd better take you home." Troy stood in the archway between the living room and the hall. He had his thumbs in his belt loops, and his shoulders slumped. He looked tired, or maybe just discouraged.

"Oh, uh, sure." Trish grabbed her purse from the coffee table. "I'll wait outside while you two say good-night."

Troy didn't speak until the door closed behind her, then looked at Marlee. "I'm sorry about tonight. About the scene with the cop."

"It wasn't your fault." She began clearing dishes from the coffee table—a half-empty popcorn bowl and two empty glasses.

"I shouldn't have been speeding," he said. "And you shouldn't have had to go through that."

His apology annoyed her. Why should he be responsible for a cop's bad attitude? "Is that what you're going to remember most about this evening— that you got a speeding ticket?" She shoved a sofa cushion back into place and picked a throw pillow up off the floor.

"Of course not. But I wanted this evening to be special—perfect."

She straightened and turned to him. "Tonight *was* special," she said softly. "It didn't have to be perfect, too."

He crossed the room and gathered her in his arms. "I love you," he whispered. "I never stopped loving you." He kissed her, an urgent, fierce kiss, full of passion and need, but lacking the lingering closeness she craved. He released her abruptly and turned away. "I'd better go."

She watched him walk out the front door. She knew she should be happy that they'd taken a huge personal step, but instead, she felt confused and uncertain. At a time when she should have been ready to return Troy's love and trust, the reminders of what life with a man with a criminal record would be like made her fearful of letting things go any further.

CHAPTER ELEVEN

BY MONDAY, Troy had convinced himself he was making too much of the incident with the cop Saturday night. So he'd been pulled over for speeding; that was no great crime.

He'd dutifully reported everything to Bernie this morning—though it grated to have to account for everything he did. That would end soon enough, as long as he stayed out of trouble and convinced the state he was no threat. In a year or two he'd be a private citizen, free to come and go as he pleased. Free to love Marlee and Greg without a cloud of suspicion hanging over him.

This optimism stayed with him until shortly after lunch, when he looked up from rebuilding a carburetor and saw Frank Britton standing in the doorway of the garage.

Troy hurriedly turned away, but not before Frank saw him. "Hey, Denton," he said. He headed toward Troy's workbench, his thin legs covering ground quickly. "Scotty around?" he asked.

"No, not today." Troy hadn't asked if Scotty had called in sick or just hadn't bothered to show up.

Lately the young con had seemed restless and Troy suspected he'd soon be moving on. Troy hoped he'd do so without making trouble.

"You talk to him this weekend?" Frank asked. "Know what he was up to?"

"I didn't. We work together—we don't hang out." *I spent the weekend with your daughter.* What would Frank say to that?

"I thought you two were pals," Frank said.

"You thought wrong."

"He said he knew you inside."

Troy glanced around, thankful no customers were close enough to hear. "We ran into each other. He needed a job and I helped him get on here. End of story." He was sorry now he'd made the effort. Scotty complained about the work, the low pay and the hours. As if bumming in the park—or sleeping in a cell—was better.

"So you don't know where I could find him? Who he hangs out with or anything?"

"No." Troy pretended to focus on the carburetor, but he watched Frank out of the corner of his eye. He could see the resemblance to Marlee in the fine cheekbones and the narrow, straight nose—though Frank's had obviously been broken more than once. Despite his anger over the way the older man had hurt her, Troy was fascinated with Frank. Why had he chosen a life of crime over one spent with a family who loved him?

"So what were you in for?" Frank asked.

At one time asking such a question in prison was

an invitation for a shiv in the back or a fist in the face. But these days computers made everyone's record available to almost anyone. If a convict didn't have access to the Internet, his friends on the outside did. Now only child molesters and perverts tried to keep their crimes secret inside.

But this wasn't prison, Troy reminded himself. "None of your business," he said.

Frank shrugged. "Just making conversation. I'm guessing nothing large. You don't have the look of a man who was inside for long."

"Long enough." He knew the look Frank was talking about—a worn, nervous awkwardness that clung to men who'd been behind bars so long they could never be completely comfortable with freedom.

"Me, too," Frank said. "I did my time and I ain't going back."

"Yeah, right," Troy said. How often had Frank said that before?

"I mean it," Frank said. "I'm not going to be one of those sorry old men who spend their last days on a cot in the prison infirmary. I used to see 'em hauled out after they passed. Saddest way I can think of to end."

Did Frank think he'd have another kind of end now? "Do you have family?" Troy asked, to see what the old man would say.

"I got a daughter somewhere. She don't speak to me, but maybe that'll change."

"Maybe she figures since you weren't around while she was growing up she doesn't owe you anything."

Frank shifted from one foot to the other. "I can see how she'd feel that way. But back then I didn't look at it any differently than if I'd had a job that took me away a lot, like a soldier or an oil-field worker."

"Except nobody has to be ashamed to admit their father is away serving his country or roughnecking in the oil fields."

"Yeah, well—I didn't say I was *right* to think that way, only that I did. And I've got an honest job now. One she wouldn't have to be ashamed of."

"I read the article in the paper," Troy said. "You're a caretaker at an apartment building?"

"Manager. I get to live there free in exchange for showing the empty places and collecting rent, calling the plumber when a toilet backs up, that kind of thing."

The woman Frank had saved in the fire had lived in one of the units in his complex.

"So you don't know where I can find Scotty?" Frank asked.

"No."

Frank frowned. "He came around to my place last week, said he had an idea how we could make some easy money."

"I don't want to hear this." Troy picked up a rag to wipe his hands and moved away.

Frank followed. "I told him I wasn't interested."

"And now you've changed your mind?" Troy shook his head. "Leave me out of this."

"You got me wrong. I'm keeping my nose clean."

"Then why do you need Scotty?"

Frank looked away, his expression shuttered. "I want to talk to him about another matter."

Troy picked up a wrench. "I have work to do."

"Yeah, sure." Frank took a step back. "If you see Scotty, tell him to give me a call."

"Leave a message with the office." He wasn't going to play go-between for Scotty and Frank. He wouldn't be caught in the middle of whatever trouble they were planning.

"Yeah, well, thanks anyway. It was good talking to you."

Troy said nothing. Though maybe talking to Frank had been good for him, too. Seeing the older man had reinforced his resolve never to end up in the same shape. Frank thought dying in prison was the worst thing that could happen to a man, but Troy knew ending up estranged from everyone you'd ever loved, with no one but yourself to blame, was almost as bad.

TUESDAY MORNING Marlee plucked a newly printed form from the printer tray and tore it in half. The pieces drifted into the recycling bin, joining the two other forms she'd already ruined. She sighed. She'd better give up on those for now. This morning was clearly meant for filing or some other task that took only half her brain. The other half was full of thoughts of Troy.

She felt a surge of desire rush through her. The memory of Troy's body against hers, his mouth caressing her, his hands stroking her, had left her restless and edgy all weekend. That one evening in his arms had whetted her appetite for him. Though he'd spent a few hours with her and Greg Sunday afternoon, they'd had no opportunity for more than a brief stolen kiss while their son was in the other room. Now she craved him, needed to see him.

At seventeen, she'd given herself to Troy the first time, and learned to love him with her body. Time had matured not only their bodies, but their minds. The love she felt now—did she even dare to call it love?—burned inside her, so deeply and intensely, it threatened to overwhelm all other feeling.

On her way to the filing cabinet, she passed the flower arrangement he'd sent this morning. Seven pink roses and a single red bud. One rose for each of the years they'd spent apart, and a bud holding the promise of a beautiful flower. She lingered in front of the vase, inhaling the subtle perfume. Red roses meant true love and passion. Troy was asking her to believe his love was true, and she wanted to. Oh, she wanted to.

So why did she have doubts? She turned her back on the flowers and resolutely made her way to the filing cabinet. As usual, the box labeled To Be Filed was overflowing. She grabbed a stack from the top and began thumbing through it.

After she and Troy had made love, she'd told herself his past didn't matter. All she cared about was that he'd come back to be a father to Greg and a partner to her.

Then the policeman had pulled them over and she'd seen him change before her eyes. She'd realized in that moment how much she *didn't* know about this man she was falling in love with all over again. And how much his past could affect their future. Had Troy really put prison behind him? How often had her father vowed to do so and failed?

The edge of a glossy sheet of paper caught her eye amid the pile of letters and carbonless forms. She slid a catalog from the stack and stared at the gleaming silver-and-blue motorcycle on the cover. A rugged-looking man straddled the bike, smiling into the camera, while a curvaceous blonde held on behind him. She thought of how it had felt to ride behind Troy, arms wrapped around him as they flew over the pavement.

"I've been looking for that. Where did you find it?" Mr. Morgenroth stopped in front of her and nodded at the motorcycle catalog.

She handed it to him. "It was in the papers to be filed."

He nodded absently and began flipping through the catalog. "Here. Tell me what you think." He opened to a two-page spread of gleaming motorcycles, crouched like panthers against a starting line. He pointed to a hulking bike loaded with chrome and leather. "That one."

She looked at the picture and tried to imagine Mr. Morgenroth racing down the freeway. She bit back a smile. "Is this the one you're buying?"

Her boss studied the picture, a dreamy expression on his face. "Maybe. Troy thought I'd like that, or maybe the Royal Star." He smiled at her. "He's been wonderful, answering all my questions and steering me in the right direction."

Troy again. Would everything today lead back to him? She busied herself straightening the papers in her hands. "So you two have become friends?"

"I *have* been spending a lot of time out at Wiley's." He chuckled. "My wife says she always knows where to find me now." He dropped the catalog onto his desk and frowned thoughtfully. "I'll admit I had my doubts about Troy that first day he came in here. I thought he looked…rough."

She nodded. "I remember. But now you've changed your mind?"

"I guess I overreacted a little because of my concern for you." Mr. Morgenroth smiled. "I'm sure it's no secret that I have a soft spot for you, Marlee. I've always thought of you almost like one of my daughters."

She flushed. "I…I'm flattered," she stammered.

"Oh, don't be. My three *real* daughters will tell you I'm far too overprotective."

She swallowed the sudden lump in her throat. *Dear Mr. M. If you only knew…* "I…I don't see much of my own father," she said.

"My dear, why not?" He shook his head. "Of course, it's none of my business. Forgive me for prying. Though if you need someone to talk to…"

Marlee shrugged. "There isn't anything to talk about. He wasn't around very often when I was a child. I haven't seen him in years."

"I imagine that would be hard." Mr. Morgenroth

took a deep breath. "Well, I can't put myself in your shoes, but as a man who's about to become a grandfather for the second time, I will say that your father is definitely missing out, not having a relationship with you and your son. Maybe…well, maybe you can still mend the rift. People do change, you know."

She shook her head. Every time her father had come home from prison when she was a child, he'd vowed to make a fresh start. He'd always ended up with his old friends, picking up the same bad habits. After a while, instead of quitting his life of crime, he'd simply quit coming home. Marlee and her mother had heard from him occasionally, but he never lived with them again. As far as Marlee was concerned, he'd made his choice years ago.

"Well, we'd better get back to work." Mr. Morgenroth stood and pulled a pair of tickets from his shirt pocket. "I wanted to talk to you anyway. I have a pair of tickets to the Ice Bats game tomorrow night, but Alice and I are going to be out of town. Maybe you'd like them instead. You and Troy could go."

She started to tell him to give the tickets to Trish or Nancy. A hockey game wasn't her idea of a romantic date. "Greg's crazy about the team," she said, hesitating.

"You can probably pick up an extra ticket at the box office and take him along."

Or Troy could take Greg. Greg would love that. She hugged the stack of papers to her chest. She hadn't yet allowed Troy to take his son anywhere by himself. But she couldn't believe he'd do anything to harm the boy.

She nodded. "I'd love the tickets, Mr. Morgenroth. Thank you." This would be her gift to Troy and Greg. And to herself. She had to learn to trust Troy. A hockey game was as good a place as any to start.

"I WONDERED IF YOU'D like to go to the hockey game tomorrow night."

Troy's grip tightened on the phone receiver. Marlee had called him at work for the first time—and she was asking him out. "Yeah. That'd be great. I didn't know you liked hockey." When he'd known her before, Marlee had been uninterested in sports of any kind.

"I don't. But Greg's a huge fan of the Ice Bats. Their mascot visited his school last year and he's been dying to go to a game ever since. And since Mr. Morgenroth gave me tickets…"

"You'd let me go with Greg—just the two of us?"

"Yes. I think it's time. Don't you?"

"Yes." He'd hoped she'd trust him enough to do this a long time ago. But he knew what a big step this was for her. "Thank you," he added.

"I got the flowers," she said, her voice softer. "They're beautiful. Thanks."

He shrugged even though he knew she couldn't see him, and shoved his free hand into his pocket. "I just thought… They made me think of you."

An awkward silence stretched between them. Marlee took a deep breath. "The game starts at seven. Why don't you come over about six?"

"Okay." They said goodbye, then he hung up and

stood staring at the phone. It was an old-fashioned black model with a rotary dial, the plastic smudged from years of mechanics' greasy hands. One day, he'd have a job that kept his hands clean. He wasn't sure exactly what he wanted to do yet; something to help people. Something to make Marlee and Greg proud of him.

"So, was that your girlfriend?"

He looked up as Scotty strolled into the office, a sheaf of invoices in his hand. Scotty deposited the invoices in a tray on Wiley's desk, then plopped into the chair. "How's Marvelous Marlee doing?"

"She's just marvelous." He hadn't told Marlee about Scotty's nickname for her.

"If I had me a woman like that, I'd be happy as a pig in slop."

Troy didn't want to talk about Marlee with Scotty. "Frank Britton came by here looking for you yesterday," he said instead.

"I know. He left a message for me."

"You two hanging out together now?"

"Not exactly."

When Scotty didn't elaborate, Troy shrugged and started to turn away.

"I tried to be friends with the old man," Scotty said. "He's got a pretty sweet setup there in that apartment building. He has the keys to all the apartments and everything. Can you believe they gave a guy like Frank that kind of access?"

"That doesn't say much for their security," Troy admitted. If management had run even a cursory background check they'd have discovered Frank had a long record. Did they really think he was just a harmless old man?

Scotty picked up a pencil and tapped it on the desktop. "He said I smelled like trouble." He laughed. "I told him that was my new aftershave."

Maybe Frank had gained a little wisdom over the years. "Is he right?" Troy asked. "Are you looking for trouble?"

Scotty's gaze slid away. "Not me, man." He tossed the pencil onto the desk. "Though I'm sure as hell tired of working this job for crap wages."

"Nobody's making you stay."

"Yeah, well, I'm just here until something better comes along."

Troy had found his something better, with Marlee and Greg. Nothing else mattered—not a job or where he lived or what other people thought of him—now that he had them back in his life.

"MAMA! HE'S HERE!"

Marlee didn't need Greg to alert her to Troy's arrival. She'd already heard the throb of the motorcycle engine. She raced to the front window in time to see the bike coast into the driveway. She caught her breath as she watched Troy dismount and pull the helmet off his head. He reached his hands in the air and stretched, a languid movement that sent a flush of heat over her.

He sauntered up the walk to the door. She stepped back from the window, but continued to watch him.

What woman wouldn't? He was the kind of man women fantasized about, all taut muscle sheathed in black leather, the danger tempered by the possibility of tenderness.

For Marlee, the danger—and the tenderness— were no fantasy. She only hoped her physical desire for Troy hadn't overwhelmed her common sense. She wanted to do what was right for herself and for Greg.

"We're going to see the Ice Bats! We're going to see the Ice Bats!" Greg opened the door and launched himself at Troy, clinging to his hand as he chanted the good news.

"Your mom told me you were a fan. Guess she was right." Troy chuckled and lifted Greg into his arms.

A different kind of warmth swept over Marlee— love for her son, coupled with the assurance that she was doing the right thing, letting him spend an evening alone with Troy. The two of them needed this chance to get to know each other better, without her interference.

Troy turned to her. "Thanks for inviting me. Next time I see Mr. Morgenroth, I'll have to tell him thank you, too."

"He mentioned he'd been coming by the shop pretty often."

"He can't seem to make up his mind about a bike. Though, I think he was checking me out, seeing if I was okay for you."

She thought of what Mr. Morgenroth had said,

about feeling as if she were one of his daughters. She flushed. "He hasn't really been doing that, has he?"

"Let's just say I seemed to answer his questions to his satisfaction." He grinned. "And he told me a lot of things about you, too."

"What kind of things?"

"Don't worry. It's all good. Scotty's taken to calling you Marvelous Marlee."

She frowned at the mention of the ex-con. "So Scotty's still there?"

"Yes." Time for a change of subject. "If the game starts at seven, I guess we'd better get going."

Greg squirmed in Troy's arms. "Let's go. We don't want to be late."

"Take my car." Marlee pulled her keys from her pocket.

"I want to ride on the motorcycle," Greg protested.

"You'll have to wait until you're older for that," Troy said.

"And come home right after the game," Marlee said. "Remember—tomorrow's a school day."

Troy nodded and took the keys, then kissed her cheek. "Thanks," he whispered. His eyes met hers for a brief moment, communicating a depth of emotion words couldn't express.

She followed them outside and stood on the porch and waved until the car was out of the driveway and headed down the street. Then she went back inside to her strangely quiet house.

She walked down the hall to Greg's room.

She sat on the side of his unmade bed, and looked at the toys and books on the shelves. The toy motorcycle Troy had given Greg held pride of place on the bedside table. A picture the two had colored together one afternoon was tacked to the closet door. Troy had breached their little fortress, insinuating himself into their lives.

The idea of Troy sharing anything with them had terrified her at first. She'd feared he'd steal Greg's love, or even Greg himself, away from her. Now she could see how wrong she'd been. Greg could love a mother and a father.

She picked up Greg's teddy bear and hugged it. She had room to love her son *and* Troy. She wondered now if she'd ever really stopped loving him, or if she'd only sealed off that part of her heart, waiting for him to return.

The ringing doorbell startled her out of her reverie. She set aside the stuffed animal and hurried down the hall. Had Troy forgotten something?

She checked the peephole as she reached for the doorknob and froze. Two men in blue uniforms stood on her front step. For a split second she thought about pretending she wasn't home. She'd hide in the bedroom until they went away.

Don't be ridiculous, she chided herself. *You haven't done anything wrong.*

With trembling fingers, she opened the door just wide enough to peer out. "Hello?" she said.

"Marlee Britton?" The older of the two officers held out his ID for her to examine. Detective Brad Getz.

"Yes?" She stared at the identification card, the picture and letters blurring in a haze of fear and nerves.

"May we come in for a moment?" Detective Getz asked.

"What is this about?" Marlee asked.

"I'm Detective Youngfield." The second officer produced his ID. "We have a few questions for you about Troy Denton."

Numb, she led them into the living room, where she sank onto the sofa, her legs unable to support her anymore. She stared at the two policemen, saying nothing.

"Ms. Britton, do you recognize this man?" Detective Youngfield handed her a photograph. It was obviously a mug shot of a young, thin man with a hooked nose. Staring at him, Marlee felt as if a heavy weight had dropped onto her shoulders, so heavy she could scarcely remain upright.

"Do you recognize him?" the officer repeated.

She nodded. "I've heard him called Scotty." She returned the picture.

"When was the last time you saw him?" Detective Getz asked.

"A couple of weeks ago, I guess."

"Where was this?"

"At Wiley's Custom Cycles. He works there."

"With Troy Denton."

She dug her nails into her palm, fighting panic. "Yes, Troy works there. Officer, what is this about?"

"Have you heard Troy talk about Scotty any?"

"Not really." *Scotty calls you Marvelous Marlee.*

"What about this man? You know him?" Detective Youngfield handed over a second mug shot.

Marlee began to tremble, and for one awful moment she thought she might be sick right there in her living room. "That's Frank Britton," she said. "My father."

CHAPTER TWELVE

THE POLICEMEN STAYED with Marlee for another half hour, asking questions she didn't want to answer. "When was the last time you saw your father?" "Did you know he's been seen speaking to Troy Denton on at least two occasions?" "Do you think they could be friends?"

Her father and Troy—friends? A friendship he hadn't told her about? "I haven't been in touch with my father in almost ten years," she said. "We don't speak. I don't know what he's up to and I don't care."

"What about Troy Denton? Do you care about him?"

She glared at Detective Youngfield, who'd asked the question. After a few long seconds, he averted his gaze.

"We know Denton has spent a lot of time over here," Detective Getz said.

"How? Have you been watching him?" she asked.

"We're conducting an investigation. Do you know where Denton is tonight?"

"He's at an Austin Ice Bats game—with my son."

"Are you sure about that?" Detective Youngfield asked.

"My boss gave them the tickets. My son was very excited about going."

"Has Denton given you any gifts lately?" Youngfield continued. "Jewelry or art or anything like that—things someone in his position might not realistically be able to afford?"

She shook her head. Troy hadn't given her jewelry or art, only toys for Greg, flowers and… "He gave me a new washer and dryer." Where had he gotten the money for those, especially since he hadn't been working for Wiley's very long at that point?

Detective Getz stood. "Thank you, Ms. Britton," he said. "We'll be in touch if we have more questions."

Marlee followed the two men to the door. "You're not going to the Ice Bats game, are you?" she asked. "My son is there…" She swallowed panicked tears. "If you're going to arrest Troy for something, at least wait until my son isn't with him." Greg adored Troy. Seeing his hero hauled away in handcuffs would destroy her innocent boy.

"Has he committed a crime that you know of?" Detective Youngfield asked.

"No! But you obviously think he's done something wrong, asking all these questions."

"We merely need Mr. Denton to give us some information," Detective Getz said.

"Do it when Greg isn't with him," Marlee pleaded. "He's only six. You'll frighten him."

"We'll wait until your son is back home," Getz said. "If we can."

Marlee watched at the window until the patrol car had pulled away from the curb and disappeared down the street. Her neighbors were probably watching, too. Next time she saw them there would be questions—the kinds of questions her childhood neighbors had had.

What were the cops doing at your house last night? What have you done?

She wrapped her arms across her stomach and began to pace. The police hadn't come right out and said Troy was mixed up in anything, but their question about expensive gifts made it clear they thought he was. And somehow Scotty and her father were also involved.

She'd been so naive. Her father had promised to go straight before, too. He'd get a job and stay clean for a while, but then he'd start hanging out with the old crowd. Or maybe he'd see something he wanted but couldn't afford, and the next thing she knew, he'd be calling from jail, asking Mama to bring the money to bail him out.

Tears streamed down her face and she didn't bother to wipe them away. Damn Troy! He'd tricked her into loving him, when all along he was no better than her father. Oh, she hated him!

She choked back a sob and stopped pacing abruptly. Oh, God! He had Greg. Surely Troy wouldn't hurt his own son. But then, she'd been wrong about everything else so far. Why should she trust him with the one thing more precious to her than life?

The clock on the microwave showed nine-thirty. They should have been home by now. *Don't panic.* She jerked open the drawer by the telephone and pulled out the phone book. She found the listing for the Exposition and Heritage Center where the Ice Bats played and punched in the number.

"Thank you for calling the Bat Cave, home of the Ice Bats Hockey Team. The office is open ten to four daily and during Ice Bats games. For information on the Ice Bats schedule, press one. To purchase tickets, press two. For Bat Gear, press three. For directions to the Bat Cave, press four. For a directory, press five…"

She hung up the phone and sagged against the wall. The game was over. *They should have been home by now.*

"Where are they, dammit?" She slapped her palm down on the counter, rattling the dishes in the drainer. The low hum of the refrigerator was her only answer.

She couldn't just sit here waiting. She glanced at the phone book lying open on the counter, then grabbed it and flipped to the listings for taxis. If Troy wouldn't bring Greg back to her, she'd go to him.

She was waiting on the porch when the taxi pulled up. "Take me to 5303 West Bend Ridge," she told the driver as she got in.

Troy's apartment was in a nondescript complex of stuccoed buildings. Older-model cars filled the spaces in the parking lot, while children's toys and rusted barbecues crowded the balconies of each unit.

She had the taxi driver cruise slowly around the complex until she found 64D. She stared up at the darkened front windows of the second-floor apartment. "Wait here," she told the driver as she climbed out of the backseat.

Her heart thudded as she mounted the steps. She hesitated, staring at the empty balcony, then jabbed at the bell. She wasn't surprised when no one answered. Cupping her hands around her face, she peered in the window through a gap in the drapes.

The living room was dark, but a light from the adjoining kitchen was bright enough that Marlee could see that the room was empty.

Completely empty. There wasn't a stick of furniture in the room, no pictures on the walls. The little she could see of the kitchen was the same—no table and chairs, no toaster on the counter or dishes in the sink. The apartment was as bare as if it had never been occupied.

Or as if the tenant had packed up and moved away.

Fear clawed at Marlee's throat, choking off her breath, and she ran down the steps. "Take me home," she ordered the cabbie. From there she could call the police. They'd have to listen when she told them a recently released prisoner had cleaned out his apartment and left—taking her son with him.

She bit her lip, fighting tears. She had to be strong, to think of Greg's safety. Later, she'd deal with her own hurt at being betrayed once again by the man she loved.

She sat forward in the seat as they neared her

house. The taxi crested the rise and she gasped. Light spilled from the front window of her home and her car was parked in the driveway. She gripped her seat, fingers cramping as they dug into the upholstery.

When the taxi slowed at the curb, she fumbled for her wallet and shoved several bills at the cabbie, then raced up the walk. Her hands shook so badly she could hardly fit the key in the lock. But at last the lock turned and she burst into the living room.

TROY WAS SURPRISED to find the house dark when he and Greg returned from the hockey game. Maybe Marlee had gone out with Trish or another girlfriend; she probably hadn't enjoyed too many free evenings since Greg was born.

"Can we watch the report on the game on the news?" Greg asked. "I want to see that awesome goal again."

"Sure." It was probably way past the kid's bedtime, but he was reluctant to end their evening together. Marlee couldn't know what a gift she'd given him, allowing him these few hours alone with his son. He'd dreamed about this for years, in those long nights when he'd lain in his prison bunk, unable to sleep.

Greg leaned forward, intent on the television. Troy smiled. He was a good-looking kid, with Troy's dark, curly hair and Marlee's nose and chin. He was smart, too, reciting the rules of the game and even reading the players' bios out loud from the program. Troy had basked in the approving smiles of those seated near them in the stadium. One woman had even remarked on the resemblance between them. *This is my son,* he'd wanted to tell them all.

One day soon, he would tell them. He and Marlee and Greg would be a family again, the way they were meant to be.

He heard the rattle of a key in the lock and stood to welcome Marlee home. "Hey, I'm glad you're back," he said. "I was starting to get worried…" The words died on his lips. Marlee stared at him, her eyes full of suspicion and fear. Troy felt as if someone had slammed a fist into his gut.

"The Ice Bats won, Mama!" Greg said, bouncing off the sofa. "And Troy bought me a pennant and we had hot dogs and—"

Marlee's expression softened as she turned to their son. "You can tell me all about it in the morning," she said. "Right now it's time for bed."

"Aw, Mom—"

"Tomorrow's a school day. Now, off you go."

"Okay. I want to say good-night to Troy."

Troy's heart twisted. He crouched down and pulled Greg close. He wanted to hang on to the boy and never let him go. No matter how angry Marlee was, he couldn't let her take Greg away from him. "Good night," Greg said, returning the hug. "Thanks for taking me to the game."

"Thank you for coming with me." Troy choked out the words. *We'll go again soon,* he wanted to say, but he hated to make promises he might not be able to keep. Marlee was clearly not in the mood to grant him any favors right now.

He straightened and watched Greg trot down the hall, his Ice Bats pennant waving over his shoulder.

"Where have you been?" Marlee's voice was fierce but low enough that Greg wouldn't hear.

Troy turned to her cautiously. His years in prison had taught him to weigh the answer to any challenge carefully. He'd learned to study his opponent, to hoard information and never give anything away. "We went to the hockey game."

"The game ended an hour ago."

He shrugged, pretending a nonchalance he didn't feel. "Greg wanted ice cream, so we stopped. The ice cream parlor had a video game, so we played a few rounds."

She dropped her purse onto the sofa, and clenched her fists at her sides. "Did you ever consider that I might be worried sick?"

The implication that he was a threat to Greg angered him. "All right, I should have called. But this isn't about my being a little late," he said. "What else is going on?"

She glanced toward the bedrooms. Then, apparently satisfied that Greg wasn't listening, she said, "The police stopped by this evening, asking about you."

Troy felt as if someone had shot his legs out from under him. He stood, waiting for the pain, waiting to fall. But he was too numb. "What did they want?" he asked, his voice hoarse.

"They wouldn't tell me exactly—just that they were investigating something. They asked about

Scotty. And about my father." Her eyes sparked with anger. "They said the two of you were friends."

"Your father and I are *not* friends."

"But you've spoken to him. The police said they'd seen you with him."

"He came by the shop once, asking for Scotty. And Scotty and I saw him at the courthouse the day he got his award. Those were the only times I've seen him."

"So why are the police looking for you?"

"I don't know, but I haven't done anything wrong."

Marlee looked away, her expression hard, refusing to yield to his pleading.

"I'm not your father," he said. "I'm nothing like him." He reached for her arm and tried to pull her close.

She jerked out of his grasp. "Don't touch me!" She moved around to the other side of the sofa. "And don't lie to me. I don't know why I didn't see it before—you *are* like my father. Still hanging out with your pals from prison. And just like Daddy, you always have plenty of cash to wave around, money for gifts and toys—or did you steal those, too? Were you planning to take Greg, just like you've taken anything else you've wanted?"

"Take Greg?" He glared at her. "Where did you get a crazy idea like that?"

She swallowed hard, as if choking back tears. "I went by your apartment tonight when you didn't come back. There wasn't any furniture. It looked like you'd already packed up to leave."

Troy shook his head, frustration building. She was twisting the truth around to fit her own expectations. "I don't need furniture," he said. "I gave most of what I had to Scotty, to help him get settled. I plan to buy more, but I've been saving my money to take care of you and Greg. I told you before—I owe you."

"You owe me!" Her voice rose, verging on hysterical. Tears spilled from her eyes. "Greg and I don't need you. We don't *want* you."

Two steps and he was around the couch, gripping her by the shoulders. "Now you're the one who's lying." He turned her toward him. "Look me in the eye and tell me you don't need me. Tell me you don't love me."

Marlee's face contorted, the tears finally streaming down her cheeks. "It doesn't matter if I love you! I loved my father and he hurt me worse because of it." She sucked in a deep, shaky breath. "I won't put myself or Greg through that kind of misery again. Just go away!"

Troy dropped her hand and took a step back. He felt hollowed out inside, empty and aching. She'd admitted she still loved him, but love wasn't enough. Nothing he could do or say could make up for the hurt that still scarred her.

He curled his hands into fists, angry at himself, and angry at Marlee's father, who'd ruined his daughter's chances for happiness before she'd even gotten started. "All right. I'm going. But you think about one thing while I'm gone. Greg is still my son.

Nothing you do or say can change that. Do you really believe that I'd ever deliberately harm him—or you? Or are you just punishing me because you can't punish your father?" He grabbed his jacket and started for the door. "Let it go, Marlee. Just let it go. You aren't hurting your father, holding on to a grudge like this—you're only hurting us, and our family. God knows, I made a big mistake. But I've served my time. I've paid my debt. I won't let you, or anybody else, keep punishing me forever."

He slammed the door behind him and strode to his bike. He'd have to ride a long time tonight before he'd outrun the memories and the pain.

MARLEE COLLAPSED onto the couch and buried her face in her hands. For the rest of her life, she'd never forget the look on Troy's face when she'd sent him away. Even beneath the anger, his eyes told her he still loved her. Or was she imagining his love for her, wanting to believe he cared because she couldn't let go of her own feelings for him?

She thought of the Troy she had first fallen in love with, so many years ago. He'd been twenty-two, older than she was, so she'd thought he was tough and mature. But now she could see that the toughness and maturity had been a thin disguise for a touching vulnerability. She shuddered as she thought of him thrown into jail with a bunch of hardened criminals.

She raised her head and forced all thoughts of sympathy from her mind. No matter how much he protested, Marlee knew prison taught a man to think only of himself. Her father had preached a philosophy of taking as much as he could get, whenever he could get it. How could Troy have survived seven years in prison without adopting that same winner-takes-all attitude?

She couldn't afford to give in to that part of herself that missed him and still longed for him. She had to be strong for Greg's sake. She wouldn't be like her mother, who had taken her father back again and again, having her heart broken every time.

Even as she lay dying of cancer, Leigh Britton had spoken of her love for the man who had ruined her life. Marlee had listened to her mother's morphine-induced ramblings in horror. She swore then and there that she'd never put herself through that kind of torture for anyone. And she certainly wouldn't expose Greg to the pain and disappointment she'd experienced as a child.

She remembered once, when she was twelve, she'd had a part in a school program, a solo with the girls' choir. Her mother had made her a new dress and bought Marlee her first pair of panty hose. She'd felt very grown-up. Her handsome father, home for one of his longest intervals yet, had fussed over her. "You're my beautiful princess," he'd said, giving her a dazzling smile. "When I see you up on that stage, I'll burst with pride."

He never got to see her onstage. The day before the program, he was caught trying to sell stolen jewelry to an undercover cop. Marlee performed her solo with tears in her eyes. Afterward, she shut herself in her bedroom and refused to listen to her mother's pleas through the locked door.

She'd grown up that night, from a trusting little girl to a wiser young woman. She'd realized then that her father would never be any different than he was. Despite her mother's love and Marlee's adoration, despite even his own best intentions, he would always betray them.

She began to weep again. Learning the truth about Troy had opened up all the old wounds. She cried for the child she'd been and for the woman she was now. She couldn't change the past, but God help her, she wouldn't spend her life repeating the same mistakes.

"Mama? What's wrong? Why are you crying?"

Greg's voice startled her. She raised her head and saw him standing in the door to the living room, his face pinched with concern. She sniffed and rubbed her eyes with the back of her hand. "I...I'm just a little sad right now, honey. I promise I'll be all right. Go back to bed."

He shuffled over to her and put a hand on her shoulder. The gesture of comfort was almost her undoing, but she swallowed hard and tried to assume a calm expression. "What are you sad about?" Greg asked.

She opened her arms and he climbed into her lap. She'd hoped to put this moment off as long as possible, to find the right words to break the news to him. But she might as well get it over with now. "Troy won't be coming to see us for a while," she said.

He was still Greg's father, but she'd limit their contact to some legally supervised visitations. And if he *was* involved in something illegal, she'd find a way to keep him from Greg permanently. She wouldn't allow his choices to hurt their son any more than they already had.

He frowned. "But…why? I thought he liked us."

Marlee brushed the hair back from her son's forehead and sighed. "He did like us. I mean, I'm sure he does like us. But it just wouldn't be a good thing for us to spend time together anymore."

She waited for tears, but Greg merely looked at her in confusion. "How could it not be good? He's my dad, isn't he?"

All her breath left her at once. "Did he tell you that?" she managed to gasp.

Greg blushed, and he hung his head as though embarrassed. "A lady at the hockey game said I looked just like him. And I knew he really liked me, and I really liked him and…well, I just sorta figured it out." He raised his head again and stared at her. "It's true, isn't it? Troy's my dad?"

Marlee nodded, feeling weak. She hadn't counted on her son being so smart. "Yes, it's true."

He shoved himself away from her, startling her with the force of the movement. When he'd squirmed out of her lap, he stood facing her, face twisted with anger. "Why'd you send him away? He just got here and now you made him leave!"

Marlee bit her lip, determined not to lie to her son, but unwilling to let him know the truth—that his father was a criminal. She reached for him, needing to pull him close. "It's better that he's gone," she said. "You'll understand when you're older."

Greg jerked away from her. "I didn't want him to leave! I hate you!" His bare feet slapped against the floor as he fled down the hall, and the windows rattled as he slammed his bedroom door behind him.

A wave of sickness washed over Marlee. Greg didn't mean those words. He didn't really hate her—he was just hurt and upset. But they were still hard for a mother to hear.

She hugged a pillow to her stomach. Would she have sent Troy away if she'd realized Greg knew Troy was his father? Troy's parting words rang in her ears. Greg would always be his son. She could never change that.

Did she believe Troy would ever deliberately hurt her or Greg? No, she didn't. But her own father had never deliberately hurt her, either, and the pain had cut just as deep.

Troy had accused her of lashing out at him because she couldn't get back at her dad. She hugged the pillow tighter, uncomfortable with the thought. Here she was, twenty-six years old and she still felt like that twelve-year-old who'd locked herself in her room and refused to speak to anyone. She was stuck in a time warp, with no way out.

She closed her eyes and saw Troy's face, love and concern softening his anger. *Let it go, Marlee.* Could she let go of the past? Could she learn to forgive what she could never forget?

CHAPTER THIRTEEN

TROY'S FIRST INSTINCT upon leaving Marlee's house was to find Scotty and demand to know what was going on. But if Scotty was in trouble, being seen with him probably wasn't a smart move. So he decided to wait and confront him at work.

Scotty never showed up at the garage the next day, but the police did. They were waiting for Troy in Wiley's office when he arrived. He felt sick at the sight of them, but forced himself not to run away. "We have some questions for you," a detective named Getz said.

"Yes, sir." Troy glanced at Wiley, who was frowning.

"We'd like you to come down to the station with us," a Detective Youngfield said.

"Are you arresting me?" Troy asked.

"No. We just have a few questions."

"Go on," Wiley said. "You and I will talk when you get back."

So Troy accompanied the cops to the station. The interview with the police was every bit as uncomfortable as he'd expected. They grilled him for two hours about his association with Scotty and Frank, about the washer and dryer and other gifts he'd given

Marlee, and asked him to provide details of his whereabouts on specific dates. Several of those dates he'd been with Marlee, though he could tell that, as Frank Britton's daughter, she wasn't considered a credible alibi.

Finally, the officers thanked him for his time and told him he was free to go, though they warned that they might have additional questions later. Was this what the rest of Troy's life would be like—always under suspicion? Always being brought in for questioning? How could he blame Marlee for not wanting to be a part of that? Even if he proved his innocence, would he be the chief suspect next time something shady happened? Would he never be able to move on?

He should have driven back to work—provided he still had a job—but instead, Troy steered the motorcycle onto Riverside, toward the Lakeside Apartments. The police had made it clear that Frank was involved in this. Troy intended to find out exactly what was going on, and do what he could to clear his name.

He cruised slowly through the parking lot until he located the manager's office. Then he parked around back. The police were probably watching the place—and watching him—so they might have already spotted him. But if they hadn't, he didn't want his presence to be too obvious.

He found the old man with an attractive woman who was changing the locks on one of the apartments. "Grace Weathers, Weathers Locksmith," she introduced herself when it became clear that Frank wasn't going to.

"Grace is changing the locks on all the apartments," Frank explained. "No more master keys. The tenants keep their own keys and we'll use lockboxes on the empty places."

"Isn't that the way most buildings do it?" Troy asked.

"Ones with owners who aren't as cheap as the guys in charge of this joint," Frank said. "They groused about the expense of doing this, but after the rash of burglaries we've had, I convinced them it was the only way to go."

The hairs on the back of Troy's neck rose. Burglaries. He'd bet he could list the dates they'd occurred—the same dates the police had questioned him about. "Do you have a few minutes to talk?" he asked.

"Sure. Gracie, you need me for anything, you know where to find me."

The locksmith nodded and the two men retreated to Frank's apartment. It was a typical low-rent, one-bedroom space, much like Troy's. An old sofa, recliner and chair shared the living room with a metal desk and two filing cabinets.

Frank sat in the recliner and motioned Troy to the sofa. "So you're one of Scotty's friends," he said.

"He's not my friend. We work together."

"That's right. The motorcycle shop. You like that job?"

"Yeah."

"Good way to make a living, I guess."

"It's okay." Troy liked Wiley's, but as long as he stayed there, he'd be surrounded by ex-cons and suspicion.

Provided, of course, Wiley didn't fire him for being questioned about a crime. Troy remembered his talk about no second chances. "What's this about a bunch of burglaries?" he asked.

"A bunch of apartments in this complex got hit while people were out at work or in the evenings," Frank said. "The thief used a master key."

"And you haven't been fired and aren't in jail?"

To Troy's surprise, Frank laughed—a sound like a rusty pump that needed to be primed. "Only because when two of the thefts occurred I was sitting in the mayor's office, discussing the ceremony for my award. And because there are no fingerprints left at any of the crime scenes, and none of the stolen property has turned up in my apartment or with anyone I know."

Frank seemed gleeful. Was it because he thought he'd gotten away with something, or because he really was innocent?

"The police came to see me at work today," Troy said. "They had a lot of questions about you and Scotty."

"Yeah, I've gotten the third degree, too. I told them I hadn't seen the guy since I ran him off weeks ago. And I hardly know you." His eyes narrowed. "Is that why you're here—to give me a hard time about the cops?"

"I wanted to find out what you knew. Do you think Scotty is involved with these burglaries?"

"He was awfully interested in the setup with the master keys. He could have made an impression when I was distracted by something, and had a copy made."

Troy studied him, trying to read the other man's face. But years of lying made Frank less likely to slip up. "You're being straight with me?" Troy asked. "You really had nothing to do with those thefts?"

"Not a thing." Frank leaned forward, eyes boring into Troy's. "What about you? Are you and Scotty in this together, looking to make some easy money and let the old con take the rap?"

"No. I've got too much to lose to pull a stupid stunt like that."

"What have you got to lose?"

"A job. Family. My freedom."

"I remember now. Scotty said you were dating a nice girl."

"Yeah." Though who knew if Marlee would ever want to see him again.

Frank sat back. "I wouldn't be telling you any of this if I really thought you had something to do with it. When was the last time you saw Scotty?"

"Last Friday. He hasn't been back to work since." Before talking to the police, Troy had wondered if this was because Scotty had left town, or because he'd been arrested.

"I saw him yesterday. I went to a taco stand where he likes to hang out and acted friendly. Bought him a beer."

"Why'd you do that?"

"I told him about a new tenant we have, a guy who collects fancy watches and electronics. I said I never saw so much expensive stuff in one place."

Troy looked around the room. "No offense, but why would a guy who could afford all that live in a dump like this?"

"You and I know he wouldn't, but in case you haven't noticed, Scotty ain't the brightest bulb in the lamp."

"I still don't understand why you told him this story."

"I didn't tell him about the new locks."

"Ah. You're hoping he'll come back to hit the new guy's place."

"And the cops and I will catch him in the act."

"If he knows the police suspect him, will he really risk hitting another place?" Troy asked.

"I knew guys like him in the joint. They were gamblers—they couldn't resist the chance to score big."

Troy thought of himself that night with Raymond. He'd been seduced by that same greed—the fantasy of earning easy money for a single night's work. He hadn't known what the job would entail, but that hadn't really mattered. He'd seen a quick way out of his troubles and grabbed it.

"Do the police know what you're up to?"

"Gracie will tell them about the new locks. And I've got 9-1-1 on speed dial. If Scotty does try to break in, they can be here in less than five minutes."

Troy stood. "Good luck. I hope it works." For both their sakes.

"You go home and keep out of trouble. Stay with that girl of yours. It's what I should have done a long time ago."

Frank spoke so matter-of-factly, Troy wondered if there was any real regret behind his words. Or maybe the older man had lived with the sadness so long he'd become an expert at concealing it.

"IS EVERYTHING OKAY, Marlee?"

Marlee jerked her head up from the report she'd been pretending to read. Trish peered at her, clearly concerned. "I'm fine," Marlee lied. Except that her life was a mess. In the two days since she'd sent Troy away, she'd barely slept. She couldn't concentrate on anything, and was behind on her tasks at work and at home. The worst part was that Greg would hardly speak to her.

"You look a little upset, that's all," Trish said.

"I'm okay. Really." Trish was sweet to be worried, but Marlee didn't want to talk about her personal problems. Wallowing in her misery wouldn't get her anywhere. She would get through this the same way she'd survived the first time Troy left her—by living in the moment and not thinking about the past.

"Do you have the latest customer-satisfaction surveys?" she asked.

"Oh, sure." Trish looked disappointed in this

change of subject, but didn't press for more details. "They're up front. I'll get them for you."

"I'll come with you." Maybe walking around would help her focus.

The surveys, which were short, postcard-size forms departing guests were asked to complete, were stored in a drawer at the registration desk. Marlee emptied the drawer and was stacking them neatly when an Austin Police officer walked in the front door.

He wasn't the same officer who'd spoken to her before, but even so she went cold at the sight of that uniform, and shrank back. Had he come to ask more questions about Troy, or about her father? Not here! Not in front of her coworkers.

"Hello." The officer smiled and glanced at her name tag. "Marlee. I hope you can help me out."

"What is it, Officer?" Trish tucked her hair behind one ear and leaned across the counter. Marlee was grateful for Trish's flirtatiousness, which distracted the officer's attention.

"There's a car parked illegally in front of the hotel. I've got the license. Maybe you can tell me if it belongs to a guest. I'd like to give them a chance to move it before it's towed."

While Trish consulted with the officer, Marlee gathered the stack of surveys and hurried back to her office. She sank onto her chair, feeling faint. She put her head in her hands and tried to control her breathing. Maybe she was losing her mind. She'd been absolutely terrified just now, all because of a man in a uniform.

"Marlee, are you okay?" Mr. Morgenroth approached her desk. She could see the neat tassels of his loafers through her fingers as he stood in front of her. She opened her mouth to make her usual assertion that nothing was wrong. But that was ridiculous. The more honest answer would be that nothing was *right*.

Marlee lowered her hands and looked up into her boss's kind eyes. "Could we talk?" she asked.

Mr. M. led her to an empty conference room and shut the door. She sat at the long table and he pulled up a chair beside her. A great feeling of calm enveloped her. Maybe this was what she should have done all along; maybe talking about her problems would lessen their power over her.

"Tell me," Mr. Morgenroth said.

She'd thought she'd talk about Troy, the trouble he was in and how much that frightened her. But when she opened her mouth, the first subject she broached was her past because, really, the present didn't make sense without understanding what had come before.

"My father's name is Frank Britton. He's been in and out of prison my whole life," she said. "I never talked about it because I was so ashamed. And I…I thought you'd think less of me."

"I don't think less of you, Marlee," Mr. Morgenroth said quietly.

She nodded. But if he'd known about her father's record before he met her, he would have felt differently. That was the way the world worked.

"I haven't seen or spoken to my dad in almost ten years," she said. "But a couple of nights ago, two policemen came to the house, asking questions about him. I think he's in some kind of trouble again."

"I can see how that would be upsetting."

"That's not the worst part," Marlee continued. "The worst part is—the police seem to think Troy is mixed up in whatever this is. They said he'd been seen with my father and another man, an ex-convict called Scotty."

The creases on Mr. Morgenroth's forehead deepened. "I don't understand. Why would Troy be with your father and this Scotty person?"

"Troy knew Scotty from…from prison. When Troy came to the hotel that very first day, he'd just been released after serving seven years for armed robbery." It sounded so bad when she said the words out loud. "It was his only offense," she hastened to add. "He got involved with a cousin and made some stupid decisions."

"But you're worried he might be falling back into old habits," Mr. Morgenroth said, his face grim.

"I don't know what to think," she said. "He was doing so well. He was working, and was such a good father to Greg and—" She put a hand to her mouth. "I didn't mean to say that."

"I had wondered," Mr. Morgenroth admitted. "There's a resemblance between them. If Troy served seven years, Greg must have been born while he was in prison."

"Yes. I was pregnant when he was arrested and after that, I refused to have anything to do with him. I didn't want my son growing up the way I did."

"But when Troy was released, he found you."

"Yes. He swore he'd gone straight and I believed him."

"Have you talked to him since you spoke with the police?" Mr. Morgenroth asked.

"Only that night, when he brought Greg home from the Ice Bats game. He said he didn't know what they were talking about—that he'd done nothing wrong. But—I kicked him out, anyway. I was just so upset and afraid." Afraid of falling back into the kind of life she'd fought so hard to escape.

"What about your father?" Mr. Morgenroth asked. "Have you talked to him?"

"Not in ten years."

"Do you think Troy is innocent?"

"I want to believe he is. But even if he is, will this happen again? Is this the kind of thing Greg is going to be exposed to?"

"Does Greg know about Troy's past? Or about his grandfather?"

"No! I didn't tell him about the police visiting the other night, either. I just told him Troy had left and wouldn't be back."

"You don't think he'll be back? At least to see his son?"

"I don't know." In many ways, it would be easier if Troy disappeared from their lives—painful, but less messy. But she couldn't wish away the connection between father and son. "If he does come back, things won't be the same," she said.

"How is Greg taking this?"

"He's devastated. He hates me for sending Troy away." Her son's coldness to her since then hurt more than anything else. "Was I wrong to do that?" she asked. "I only wanted to protect him."

"I don't know what to tell you, Marlee." Mr. Morgenroth spread his hands in a gesture of helplessness. "It might be good to have more facts, but in the end, you're the only one who knows what you can accept. Your experiences growing up give you a different perspective than an outsider like me."

"I wish none of this had ever happened," she said. "Not my father, or Troy's arrest or any of it. I just want a normal, law-abiding life."

"You haven't broken any laws, and we don't know that Troy has, either. As for the rest…" He shrugged. "You wouldn't be the person you are today if you hadn't been through the things you have. The past is part of us."

Troy had said the same thing, hadn't he? And much as she'd tried to put her past behind her, it affected every decision she made. "I guess you're right," she said. "I made my choice, and now I have to live with it."

Mr. Morgenroth stood. "If you need to take a few days off, or if you need my help with anything, let me know," he said.

"Thanks. And thank you for listening." Talking had helped. She felt less isolated and alone than she had in a long, long time.

Mr. Morgenroth left the conference room, but Marlee stayed where she was, staring at an abstract painting on the wall and thinking about the past—and the future. Troy was still Greg's father, and sending him away hadn't really solved anything. Greg might take Marlee's word at face value now, but as soon as he was old enough to find his way around the Internet, he could learn the particulars of Troy's past—and all about his grandfather, too. Would Marlee lose her son because she'd tried to shield him from these realities?

And what if Troy was innocent? With the distance of a few days, the idea that he'd broken the law again seemed ridiculous. He'd been so determined to live a good life.

She'd been such a fool! As Mr. Morgenroth had pointed out, how could she make smart decisions when she didn't know all the facts? Instead of acting rashly and jumping to conclusions, she needed to find out what was really going on. And she needed to make peace with her past, as well. Only then could she take away the power it held over her.

TIRES CRUNCHED on gravel as Marlee pulled into the lot of Lakeside Apartments. She followed the driveway between the rows of square gray buildings and parked in front of one marked Office. She shut off the engine, then sat for a while, staring out at the neatly clipped patches of grass in front of each building.

Maybe coming here today had been a bad idea. She could start the car again and leave now. No one would ever know.

"Coward," she muttered, and shoved open her

door. She climbed three concrete steps to the office door. A note tacked to the faded blue paint said, *Out back trimming hedges. Frank.*

Marlee stared at the signature—the same flamboyant *F* and trailing *K* that had graced childhood birthday cards and his infrequent letters from prison. The sight of it brought back so many sad memories, but her eyes remained dry.

She heard a buzzing like a swarm of insects and followed it around the side of the building and across the yard to a row of hedges that marked the border of the property. An older man in baggy green coveralls and a black ball cap was operating an electric hedge trimmer, an orange extension cord trailing behind him. Her father.

He was smaller than she remembered, thin and stoop shouldered. Marlee watched him for a few minutes. Almost ten years had passed since she'd last seen him. Would they have anything to say to each other?

She took a deep breath and started toward him. She was almost at his side before he saw her. He shut off the hedge trimmers and pushed back his hat, giving her a view of his brown eyes, which looked paler now, watery.

She stopped directly in front of him. "Can I help you, miss?" he asked.

Marlee swallowed hard, hurt that he didn't recognize her. She would have known him anywhere, no matter how much time had passed. She cleared her throat. "It's me, Dad. Marlee."

Frank's gaze sharpened, pinning her. He swallowed hard, his Adam's apple bobbing. Then a softness crept into his expression. "It's good to see you, princess."

Marlee was afraid she'd be overcome before she'd had a chance to speak her piece. The surge of emotion surprised her; she'd thought she was long past feeling anything for her father, much less this sadness and yes, *tenderness* that swept over her now. "I was wondering if there was somewhere we can talk," she said.

He nodded and motioned toward a trio of picnic tables in the shade of a cedar pavilion. "Is that all right?"

She followed him to the pavilion. Beside it sat a rusted barbecue grill and a sand pit for horseshoes. "How are you doing?" she asked, sliding onto one of the picnic benches.

"I'm all right." Frank lowered himself to the bench across from her. "A friend got me the job here, and it comes with a little apartment. It's not perfect, but the location's really convenient."

Marlee stared out across the rows of shabby buildings. "I saw an article about the fire," she said. "The one where you saved that woman."

"So that's how you knew where I was." He coughed. "I tried to look you and your ma up when I got out this last time, but you'd moved."

"The rent kept going up, so we moved a few times. After Mama died, I found a place of my own."

"Leigh's gone then?" Frank sounded pained, and Marlee was surprised to see tears well in his eyes.

"I thought you knew," she said.

He looked away and sniffed. "I guess in my heart I did. It felt like I'd really lost her this time."

Marlee tried to swallow past the tightness in her throat. What would it be like to love someone so much you felt that kind of connection, even miles and years apart?

"When did it happen?" he asked.

"Two years ago. She had cancer."

He nodded, and stared off across the lawn.

Marlee didn't want to feel sorry for him. She'd kept her bitterness alive for so many years but now, confronted with the sad reality of her father's life, she couldn't feel any anger toward him. "How long have you been out?"

"Oh, almost five years now. Prison is no place for an old man."

She'd never thought of her father as old before. She raised her head and looked at him. Up close, his face had a weathered appearance, all lines and valleys. He must have been near sixty, but he looked older. What hair that showed beneath the cap was shot through with silver. "Do you miss your old friends?"

He laughed. "Well, you know, the parole board frowns on socializing. But I still see Danny Bernardo. He married a woman with three daughters about, oh, nine years ago. They run a doughnut shop over on the Drag."

She blinked. "So Danny went straight?"

He laughed again. "You sound surprised. It happens, you know. Not everybody is like your old man."

She nodded. She'd known for some time now that Troy wasn't like her father. He'd learned years ago what it had apparently taken her father decades to absorb—that crime truly *didn't* pay, and that it cost you more than you ever gained.

"So why'd you come to see me?" her father asked.

"The police paid me a visit a few days ago," she said. "They were asking about you."

His expression hardened and she realized the toughness she'd known as a child wasn't gone, merely suppressed under this new, milder exterior. "They had no right to bother you."

"What was it about?" she asked. "Are you in some kind of trouble?" *Again.*

"No." His eyes met hers, the hardness still there. "This time, I really am innocent."

She wanted to believe him, but experience made her cautious. "Then what *did* happen? Why were they asking about you?"

Frank studied the ground a moment, as if weighing what to tell her. "There's this young con, name of Scotty, who started hanging around here a couple of months ago," he said. "I didn't invite him or anything, he just showed up. I knew him inside and I felt sorry for the kid, so I had him over a few times—you know, to watch the game or grill some burgers. But he wouldn't shut up about the two of us doing a job together—finding someplace to rob. I finally ran him off, but not before he stole a master key. He used it to break into some of the apartments."

"And you knew nothing about this?"

"No. I did not."

So the police had been right about Scotty. "Do you...do you know a man named Troy Denton?"

Frank's gaze sharpened. "What about him?"

"Was he involved with Scotty in robbing the apartments?"

Frank leaned toward her. "How do you know Troy Denton?"

"First tell me if he's part of this."

"No. The cops questioned him because he works with Scotty and because they saw him talking to me—but he had nothing to do with this."

"You're sure."

"Positive. They caught Scotty red-handed last night and he had some other young punk with him."

All the anger and hurt that had held Marlee upright for the past few days drained out of her in a rush, replaced by shame and sadness.

"How do you know Troy?" her father asked again.

She scored the top of the table with her thumbnail. "I've known him for a long time. We met when I was in high school. We were going to get married, but then he was sent to prison."

Frank let out a low groan. "I should've been there," he said. "I would never have let you get involved with a con."

"Troy's not like that," she said. "He's a good man. He made a mistake and paid for it."

"So you waited for him to get out. The way your mother used to wait for me."

"No. I didn't wait. I didn't want anything to do with him."

Frank looked away. "I guess I can't blame you for that, after the way I was always letting you and your mother down."

She nodded. Even Leigh had finally accepted that her husband wouldn't change, after Marlee spent years telling her so. "But I couldn't ever really forget Troy. I...I was pregnant when he left. I have a son— Greg."

Frank blinked, mouth gone slack. "So I'm a grandpa." Marlee could hear the wonder in his voice.

"Yes. I guess you are."

He pulled off his cap and combed one hand through his still-thick hair. "So Troy got out and found you and the boy again, is that it?"

She nodded. "He told me he wanted to be a father to his son—that he wanted another chance with me, too. He said he'd stay out of trouble from now on."

"Has he done right by you since then?"

"Yes."

"Do you love him?"

"Yes, but..."

"But what?"

"But what will my life be like with him? Will the police always show up at my door with questions? Will my son be teased about his father the jailbird, the way I was? Even if we move, the information will show up on every credit check and job application. If he's ever stopped for speeding or a burned-out taillight, the local police will know."

Frank sighed. "Troy's got a job, right? He's working and giving you money? He wasn't involved in the burglaries here and he cooperated with the police. What more do you want?"

"I want to be sure."

"You can't be. You've got to follow your heart."

The answer seemed glib. "Mama followed her heart," she snapped. "Look where it got her."

Her father didn't flinch. "You only remember the bad times. Your mother wasn't like that. She focused on the good times. No matter what happened, she knew I loved her. And she loved me."

"Love isn't always enough." It hadn't been enough for Leigh in the end. She'd tried to build a new life without Frank, but it had been too late.

Frank reached across the table and laid his hand atop hers. The tattoos were still there among the wrinkles, faded now, less menacing. His fingers were rough and callused, with dirt under the nails. A picture flashed through Marlee's mind of these same fingers, nails neatly manicured, rolling a cigarette. She'd been fascinated by the process when she was a child.

"I know I wasn't much of a father, but I never stopped loving you," he said, his voice gruff. "I swore I'd make it up to you one day, but by then it was too late."

She shivered, struck by the similarity between his words and Troy's. But Troy had come back to try again, hadn't he?

"You and Troy are still young," he continued. "You can learn from this old man's mistakes."

Marlee caught her breath, the tightness in her chest easing slightly. Maybe that was all she'd really come here for—to hear him say he was wrong and he knew it. And to discover that the ties of blood and memory still bound them together, stronger than ever.

He laced his fingers with hers. "Give him another chance. And if he messes up this time, he'll answer to me."

She didn't try to stop the tears. They slid down her cheeks, splashing onto their intertwined fingers. She leaned across the table and kissed her father's cheek and felt the dampness there also. "I'm glad I found you again, Daddy," she whispered.

He patted her shoulder. "Me, too, princess. Me, too."

CHAPTER FOURTEEN

TROY DROPPED the cardboard carton on the closet floor and began tossing in clothes. Not much to pack, really. A few dishes, some books, the mattress and the bed linens, a handful of clothes. Those years in prison had taught him just how little a man needed to live. Later on, he'd have things—furniture and art and all the other small luxuries that softened life's rough edges. Right now he had more important things to spend his money on. And he still tried to put some aside for Greg and Marlee.

It would probably always hurt to think of the two of them—all the family he cared to have. *I should have fought harder to stay with her. I shouldn't have let her send me away.*

He closed the top on the box and backed out of the closet. He only needed to gather up a couple more things and he'd be ready to go.

He'd kept busy the past week, polishing his résumé and going for interviews. Wiley had written him a letter of recommendation and so had his parole officer, Bernie. After Scotty had been arrested for the thefts at Lakeside Apartments, Bernie was more ready to believe Troy's assertions that he'd straightened out his life, and promised to do all he could to help him.

Wiley had told him he could stay at the shop as long as he wanted, but Troy needed to move on.

A hard knock on his door startled him. Not many people knew where he lived. He glanced through the peephole. Marlee looked back at him, her face filling his vision, like an image from his dreams. He unlatched the chain and opened the door, fighting the impulse to pull her to him. The next move had to be hers.

She looked beyond him, into the apartment. "Can I come in?"

He stepped aside and she walked in. He caught the scent of her perfume, sweet and subtle, and followed her with his eyes as she walked into the kitchen.

He clenched his jaw and shut the door, then stalked past her. "We can talk while I finish up here." He grabbed an empty carton and headed toward the bathroom.

He opened the medicine cabinet and swept its contents into the box, then pulled a stack of towels from the shelf over the toilet. "You're packing," she said, sounding stunned.

"Yeah, well, it didn't look like you wanted anything to do with me, so I took a better offer."

"Troy, I…" She sighed. "I need to talk to you— about the other night."

He deposited a bar of soap, a razor and half a pack of toilet paper in his box. "So talk. I'm listening."

Marlee was silent, though Troy could hear her breathing, a soft and vulnerable sound. He gripped the carton, his fingers digging into the cardboard. "I went to see my father a few days ago," she said finally.

He blinked. "You did?"

"Yes. We talked."

"What about?"

"Lots of things. I told him about Mama dying, and about Greg. And about you."

"So what does he think of the man who got his daughter pregnant, then got thrown in jail? Is he on his way over here to whip my ass now?" He closed the medicine cabinet and stared into the mirror. Marlee peered over his shoulder at him, her eyes wide and dark, fearful. She had never looked so beautiful to him. Was that because he might never see her again?

"He…he thinks I should give you another chance." Her voice trembled.

Troy set the box on the sink and turned to face her. Her gaze met his, full of fear and questions. "What do *you* think?" he asked.

She hesitantly touched his wrist, her fingers like ice on his skin. "I love you, Troy. I don't want to lose you again."

He opened his arms and she stepped into the heat of his kiss. They came together fiercely, as if gentle words and touches couldn't convey the depth of their feelings. She clung to him, her face wet with tears. "Please don't go," she murmured. "I'm sorry I doubted you."

"I'm sorry I ever let you down," he said, stroking her hair. "I swear it won't happen again."

She pulled away, just enough to look at him. "Will you stay, then?"

"I wasn't going far, anyway," he said. "I got a new job."

"A new job?"

"Yeah. I'm going to be a counselor at a halfway house for ex-cons. There's a day center, and some apartments. We try to make the transition back to the free world easier. It's just part-time at first, so I'll still work at Wiley's. Once I've been there a year and completed my parole, I'll be eligible for a full-time position."

"I would have thought after your experience with Scotty, you'd be done helping ex-cons," she said.

"That's what I told myself. I wanted to forget all about prison and anything to do with it. I even wanted to leave Wiley's because I knew he'd hire other guys who'd been in prison, and I didn't want to be around them."

"What happened to change your mind?"

"It was seeing your dad, really. I liked him, in spite of what he did to you. I think maybe he's changed. Maybe softened in the past few years. If a man with a record like his can do that, maybe there's hope for others. I talked to Bernie and he helped me get on at the halfway house."

"I think you're right." Marlee sighed. "I still wish things had been different when I was growing up, but I can't keep letting the past rule my life. At least my dad and I can have some kind of relationship now, and Greg can get to know his grandfather."

"I was trying to forget the past altogether, but that's impossible. I was left with feeling sorry and guilty about something I couldn't help. So I tried to think how I could take something bad—my time in prison—and turn it into something positive. I talked with my parole officer and he recommended this counseling program. It seemed like a good fit." He squeezed her hand. "I'm going to make a difference in people's lives."

"You could make a difference in our lives, too— mine and Greg's."

"Does this mean you'll take me back?"

She nodded. "I'm sorry I ever sent you away. I was just scared."

He held her close. "I know. I can't promise we'll never be challenged or face questions again, but I promise I won't let you down."

"And I won't let you down," she said. "I'm sorry for running out on you when you were convicted. I was scared, but I was wrong. I won't do that again."

Troy loosened his hold and stepped back slightly. "We have to tell Greg that I'm his dad. Right away."

"He already knows. He figured it out all by himself."

"And he's okay with that?"

"Are you kidding? He's crazy about you."

Relief washed over him. "I knew he was a smart kid." He smoothed his hands down her shoulders. "As soon as we can, we'll file the papers to make it official."

"I've made some other decisions recently," she said.

Was that a hint of a smile at the corners of her mouth? "What kind of decisions?" he asked.

"I signed up for that mentoring program at work. I'll fly to Saint Louis at the end of the month for a week of training, then I'll be paired up with a mentor here in Austin—probably at the North Crowne Towers."

"You'll be meeting a lot of new people."

"Yes. And part of me is terrified, but the rest…" Marlee shrugged. "I think I was wrong to shut other people out of my life for so long. Keeping secrets didn't protect me—it only gave those secrets more power over me."

"You'll do great in the program," he said. "And if you need me to look after Greg anytime, you know I will."

She glanced past him, at the boxes stacked around the apartment. "Are you going to live at the halfway house?"

"For a while. Figured I'd save more money for Greg's college fund."

"You could live with us. Greg would like that. *I'd* like it."

"You're sure?"

"I'm sure." Her gaze was steady and unblinking. "I love you, Troy. More than ever."

"I love you, too." He clasped her hands in his and spoke the same words he'd said seven years earlier. "Marlee Britton, will you marry me?"

He could see the shock on her face. "Marry you?"

He nodded. "I told you, I want to do everything right this time."

"I always thought happily ever after was make-believe," she said.

"It's only make-believe if you think happiness happens all by itself, with no work on your part." He squeezed her shoulder. "What do you say, Marlee? We've spent so much time worrying about the past. Let's work on the future—together. I don't believe in fairy tales any more than you do, but I know we can be happy together."

The smile he'd glimpsed earlier found its way to her lips now. "So do I," she said. She kissed him, a lingering, soul-searing caress that left him dizzy. "Yes, I'll marry you," she breathed when at last they parted. "And we *will* be happy together. I've never wanted anything more."

"You're all I ever wanted," he said. "You and our son." A family at last.

* * * * *

*Fan favorite Leslie Kelly is bringing her readers a
fantasy so scandalous,
we're calling it FORBIDDEN!*

*Look for
PLAY WITH ME.
Available February 2010 from
Harlequin® Blaze™.*

" AREN'T YOU GOING TO SAY 'Fly me' or at least 'Welcome Aboard'?"

Amanda Bauer didn't. The softly muttered word that actually came out of her mouth was a lot less welcoming. And had fewer letters. Four, to be exact.

The man shook his head and tsked. "Not exactly the friendly skies. Haven't caught the spirit yet this morning?"

"Make one more airline-slogan crack and you'll be walking to Chicago," she said.

He nodded once, then pushed his sunglasses onto the top of his tousled hair. The move revealed blue eyes that matched the sky above. And yeah. They were twinkling. Damn it.

"Understood. Just, uh, promise me you'll say 'Coffee, tea or me' at least once, okay? Please?"

Amanda tried to glare, but that twinkle sucked the annoyance right out of her. She could only draw in a slow breath as he climbed into the plane. As she watched her passenger disappear into the small jet, she had to wonder about the trip she was about to take.

Coffee and tea they had, and he was welcome to them. But her? Well, she'd never even considered making a move on a customer before. Talk about unprofessional.

And yet…

Something inside her suddenly wanted to take a chance, to be a little outrageous.

How long since she had done indecent things—or decent ones, for that matter—with a sexy man? Not since before they'd thrown all their energies into expanding Clear-Blue Air, at the very least. She hadn't had time for a lunch date, much less the kind of lust-fest she'd enjoyed in her younger years. The kind that lasted for entire weekends and involved not leaving a bed except to grab the kind of sensuous food that could be smeared onto—and eaten off—someone else's hot, naked, sweat-tinged body.

She closed her eyes, her hand clenching tight on the railing. Her heart fluttered in her chest and she tried to make herself move. But she couldn't—not climbing up, but not backing away, either. Not physically, and not in her head.

Was she really considering this? God, she hadn't even looked at the stranger's left hand to make sure he was available. She had no idea if he was actually attracted to her or just an irrepressible flirt. Yet something inside was telling her to take a shot with this man.

It was crazy. Something she'd never considered. Yet right now, at this moment, she was definitely considering it. If he was available…could she do it? Seduce a stranger. Have an anonymous fling, like something out of a blue movie on late-night cable?

She didn't know. All she knew was that the flight to Chicago was a short one so she had to decide quickly. And as she put her foot on the bottom step and began to climb up, Amanda suddenly had to wonder if she was about to embark on the ride of her life.

Sold, bought, bargained for or bartered

He'll take his...

Bride on Approval

Whether there's a debt to be paid,
a will to be obeyed or a business
to be saved...she has no choice
but to say, "I do"!

PURE PRINCESS, BARTERED BRIDE
by *Caitlin Crews*
#2894

Available February 2010!

www.eHarlequin.com

HP12894

LARGER-PRINT BOOKS!
GET 2 FREE LARGER-PRINT NOVELS PLUS
2 FREE GIFTS!

HARLEQUIN®

Super Romance

Exciting, emotional, unexpected!

YES! Please send me 2 FREE LARGER-PRINT Harlequin® Superromance® novels and my 2 FREE gifts (gifts are worth about $10). After receiving them, if I don't wish to receive any more books, I can return the shipping statement marked "cancel." If I don't cancel, I will receive 6 brand-new novels every month and be billed just $5.44 per book in the U.S. or $5.99 per book in Canada. That's a saving of over 15% off the cover price! It's quite a bargain! Shipping and handling is just 50¢ per book in the U.S. and 75¢ per book in Canada.* I understand that accepting the 2 free books and gifts places me under no obligation to buy anything. I can always return a shipment and cancel at any time. Even if I never buy another book from Harlequin, the two free books and gifts are mine to keep forever.

139 HDN E4JY 339 HDN E4KC

Name	(PLEASE PRINT)	
Address		Apt. #
City	State/Prov.	Zip/Postal Code

Signature (if under 18, a parent or guardian must sign)

Mail to the **Harlequin Reader Service:**
IN U.S.A.: P.O. Box 1867, Buffalo, NY 14240-1867
IN CANADA: P.O. Box 609, Fort Erie, Ontario L2A 5X3

Not valid for current subscribers to Harlequin Superromance Larger-Print books.

**Are you a current subscriber to Harlequin Superromance books and want to receive the larger-print edition?
Call 1-800-873-8635 today!**

* Terms and prices subject to change without notice. Prices do not include applicable taxes. N.Y. residents add applicable sales tax. Canadian residents will be charged applicable provincial taxes and GST. Offer not valid in Quebec. This offer is limited to one order per household. All orders subject to approval. Credit or debit balances in a customer's account(s) may be offset by any other outstanding balance owed by or to the customer. Please allow 4 to 6 weeks for delivery. Offer available while quantities last.

Your Privacy: Harlequin Books is committed to protecting your privacy. Our Privacy Policy is available online at www.eHarlequin.com or upon request from the Reader Service. From time to time we make our lists of customers available to reputable third parties who may have a product or service of interest to you. If you would prefer we not share your name and address, please check here. ☐

Help us get it right—We strive for accurate, respectful and relevant communications. To clarify or modify your communication preferences, visit us at www.ReaderService.com/consumerchoice.

HSRLP10

HARLEQUIN® *Blaze*™

*It all started
with a few naughty books....*

As a member of the Red Tote Book Club,
Carol Snow has been studying works of
classic erotic literature…but Carol doesn't
believe in love…or marriage. It's going to take
another kind of classic—Charles Dickens's
A Christmas Carol—and a little otherworldly
persuasion to convince her to go after her
own sexily ever after.

Cuddle up with

Her Sexy Valentine

by STEPHANIE BOND

Available February 2010

---

red-hot reads

HARLEQUIN® HISTORICAL:
Where love is timeless

Whirlwind Secrets
DEBRA COWAN

HE *WILL* UNCOVER
THE TRUTH!

Russ Baldwin has learned from harsh experience
to look twice at people. When his business partner,
Miss Lydia Kent, moves into town, he goes
on high alert....

Russ's watchful eyes rattle Lydia. She must keep
her noble, yet underground, activities—and
her emotions—tightly under wraps. When Russ
realizes his curvy, sweet-talkin' co-owner has
hidden depths, he's determined to uncover them!

*Available February
wherever you buy books.*

www.eHarlequin.com

HH29579